"I have had the pleasure of reading *Whale Island and the Mysterious Bones*, a wonderful children's adventure story and a feast for young imaginations. The story is well-drawn with very believable and sympathetic characters. The plot has the reader turning pages quickly to find out what happens next to the protagonists, Katey, Will and Uncle Hughie. The antagonists, Captain Sharkley and Henshaw keep our heroes on their toes, racing one step ahead of the dastardly fates intended for them. From wild storms, to kidnapping and shark attacks, the main characters finally make their way to a magical place; Whale Island. It is here where Karen L. Bonnet's talent as a writer really shines, capturing the reader with her descriptive paragraphs—both beautiful and enticing. Readers will want to have more stories about Katey, Will and Uncle Hughie. On a personal note I have worked with Karen and she is a creative professional who maintains her integrity as a writer and in her promotional work."

—Linda Maria Frank, Author of The Madonna Ghost *and* Girl With Pencil Drawing, *Massapequa, NY*

"Mrs. Bonnet captured the hearts and imaginations of my twenty-five third graders in 2006, as she charted them on a journey into a world where an undersea kingdom offered treasures and surprises. Each new adventure of Katey and Will left us at the edge of our seats, hungry for the next word. We traveled with them holding our breaths, fearful for Uncle Hughie; riveted, and waiting to discover the mysteries of the Island. We wondered whether they all would ever find their way back home. Through the careful crafting of language and development of character, Mrs. Bonnet creates a rich, visual excursion with characters that are believable and familiar, with places that we could actually paint because they are described with lush sensory descriptions. I cannot wait to open the pages of *Whale Island and the Mysterious Bones*, and enchant my next group of third graders with the adventure."

—*Denise Kass, third grade teacher, Oceanside School #5*

"I thoroughly enjoyed *Whale Island and the Mysterious Bones*, which is full of adventure. I know that children will find themselves caught up in the fun and suspense right to the end."

——*Shirley Rugolo, Oceanside, New York*

"Besides providing a child with a book to love, my greatest reward as a librarian has been encouraging aspiring writers. When Karen approached me two years ago with her manuscript and asked me to read it, I was delighted to be part of the creative process. Because I read so many books for children and young adults, I knew that Karen's story had the potential to be a riveting middle school novel. It has been my pleasure to be some help in the birth of *Whale Island and the Mysterious Bones*."

——*Barbara Buckley, Head of Children's Services, Oceanside Library*

"This remarkable story immediately took me back to a simpler, more innocent time in life. As I journeyed along with the characters, I couldn't help but feel the sincerity, strength, vulnerability, passion and love for family these characters displayed which will make this timeless story an instant favorite of children and adults alike."

—*Kathy McBride-Ferran, Glendale, NY*

WHALE ISLAND

AND THE
MYSTERIOUS BONES

WHALE ISLAND

AND THE MYSTERIOUS BONES

Karen Bonnet

Legwork Team Publishing
New York

Legwork Team Publishing
80 Davids Drive, Suite One
Hauppauge, NY 11788
www.legworkteam.com
Phone: 631-944-6511

Disclaimer:
This book, intended for young readers, is for educational and entertainment purposes only. The story, its characters and entities are fictitious. Any likeness to actual persons, either living or dead, is entirely coincidental.

The ideas expressed herein are solely those of the author and do not necessarily reflect or represent those of Legwork Team Publishing or its staff. The publisher makes no endorsement as to the utility of this work and accepts no responsibility for reader conclusions, actions or results.

First edition 01/24/2011

Printed in the United States of America
This book is printed on acid-free paper

Illustrated by Francis A. Bonnet
www.francisbonnet.com
Designed by Vaiva Ulenas-Boertje

Legwork Team
Publishing

For my husband, Lou;
my children, Francis, LeeAnne, Jacqueline, and Jonathan
—they hold a special place in my heart;
and most especially to my granddaughter, Katelyn,
who brings me endless joy.

Every trial endured and weathered in the right spirit
makes a soul nobler and stronger than it was before.
—James Buckham

There never was any heart truly great and generous
that was not also tender and compassionate.
—Robert Frost

Great men are they who see that spiritual is stronger
than any material force—that thoughts rule the world.
—Ralph Waldo Emerson

The best and most beautiful things in the world cannot be seen
or even touched—they must be felt with the heart.
—Helen Keller

CONTENTS

PREFACE

Everyone has a story to tell. Talk to any person about an experience in their lives which inspired or had great significance to them, and an interesting, unique story unfolds.

This adventure book was woven out of events and experiences from my past—friends and family that touched my life—and through reading the books I loved, which influenced me as a reader and writer. *Whale Island and the Mysterious Bones* is for the young, and the young-at-heart, and for anyone who has learned, or should learn, that courage lies in those who face their fears head on, even when they're afraid.

Each of us needs to continue to learn, love, explore, pursue our dreams, and to find new adventures to ensure a fulfilling, meaningful life. Enjoy the journey.

ACKNOWLEDGMENTS

My sincere gratitude and love is extended to all my devoted friends and family members for taking time to read my book when it was in its infant stages, and even after I edited it hundreds of times. Their comments, words of praise, and encouragement were stimuli to my imagination so that words to the story continued to pour freely during the writing process.

Heartfelt thanks and much love to my talented son, Francis Bonnet, whose artistic skills in illustration turned the front pages of my book into something beautiful and eye-catching.

Many, many thanks to my cousin, Kathy Ferran; friends, Patricia Donnelly, Beebee Martin, Shirley Rugolo, Chris Scarangella, and Brian Klose, the first youngster to read the book in manuscript form. I will never forget Brian, an involved youngster, who assisted me by providing feedback at a time when he was busy with homework, school, and afterschool activities.

ACKNOWLEDGMENTS

Thank you from the bottom of my heart to my parents, Estelle and Frank O'Brien whose love, guidance, and wisdom shaped who I am today; to my husband's wonderful, loving parents, Raymunda and Augusto Bonnet; to Aunt Flory, my favorite aunt; Uncle Terry, my favorite uncle, and all my cousins—you were and still are such an important part of my life. Thanks for the memories.

For my brother, Mickey, (who is much like the protagonist, Will)—it is true that our young minds and vivid imaginations in the games we invented, played a part in the creation of this story. To my sister, Dorothy Senay, who will always be close to my heart; my nephews, Louis and Billy Senay; and my niece, Stephanie Bonnet—I am forever grateful to you for sharing your thoughts and feelings about my book.

My sincere appreciation and admiration to the late Susan Satriano, a dear friend, whose courage, gentle spirit and compassion were an inspiration to me and to many others.

I will forever be grateful to Mrs. Barbara Buckley, children's librarian at Oceanside Library who enjoyed my book and lifted my spirits after she told me it was a "page turner and a very exciting story." Her sound advice and words of encouragement helped me tremendously.

To Mrs. Denise Kass and her entire 2006 third grade class at Oceanside School #5, whose enthusiasm for the story touched me to my very soul—your genuine interest, paintings depicting scenes in the story, and gift of flowers were beautiful. I will always remember those extraordinary moments, just as if it happened yesterday.

I would be remiss if I did not acknowledge the dedicated efforts of Yvonne Kamerling and Janet Yudewitz of Legwork Team Publishing. I extend my gratitude to them, and as the name implies, their team of design, editorial and technical professionals for transforming my story into the book you hold in your hands.

In closing, I would like to thank God for the many blessings He has bestowed on me and my loved ones.

INTRODUCTION

Katelyn Sarah Longley was daydreaming again. In her mind's eye, she remembered Whale Island. Her thoughts drifted with memories as she conjured up vivid images about the island, a strikingly beautiful land located thousands of miles away from her home. It was there that she and her brother, Will, discovered adventure and danger that changed their lives forever. Oh, how she would love to go back in time!

Whale Island was a home to huge animals and plants not seen anywhere else, and one of many small islands in Indonesia that stretched for miles and miles. There were larger-than-life Komodo dragons that looked like small dinosaurs, and the whales, dolphins, and fish were also quite extraordinary in more ways than one could imagine! The animals that roamed the vast landscape, which was abundant with flowers, thick lush plants and trees, were truly the most spectacular Katey and Will had ever seen. Even so, at times, the unusual animals they encountered struck fear in Katey's heart. She recalled the time a Komodo dragon nearly killed her friend, George, and she shuddered, a chill working its way up her back.

It was six months since she and Will returned from their unusual journey, but to Katey, it seemed as if an eternity had passed. She remembered the day it all began, with Uncle Hughie at the helm of his new boat, and their choppy ride to Green Cave Island, a small inlet not far from home. When she and Will stepped into Uncle Hughie's boat, they never expected their lives would soon be turned upside down. She and Will thought they would never see their father again.

Katey watched the snow gathering on the window ledge as she recalled that unforgettable moment in time, the last day of school—June 24, 2006.

CHAPTER 1

THE LAST DAY OF SCHOOL

It was a sweltering June morning—the first day of summer and last day of school for the children who lived in Barnstable, Massachusetts. Katey's eyes were glued on the hands of the clock, as if it would help time move faster. She could hardly contain her excitement knowing that Uncle Hughie would be meeting her and Will after school. He was bringing *Dotty*, his new fishing boat, so they could ride along the Cape Cod Bay coastline. She looked out the window at the bay beyond and turned to catch the golden sunlight flickering on a sea of waves. She felt her body relax, the sun warming her face.

Closing her eyes, she imagined how it would feel to be on the boat, with the sea in front of them for miles and miles. Mesmerized by the peaceful scene in her mind, she barely heard the murmur of children's voices in the background. *The waves seem to be doing an endless dance*, she thought dreamily, as her eyes slowly fluttered open. She wished she could run down by the water where ripples of tiny waves met the shoreline. A hint of a smile played on her lips as she watched the downward flight of a seagull descending into the water from the cloudless, bright blue sky. Wings outstretched gracefully, the brown and white bird landed on the water's surface without so much as making a splash.

Just as if he was standing right before her, Uncle Hughie's face popped into Katey's head. She was impatient for the day to end, as she was sure that this fishing trip would lead them to new discoveries. Uncle Hughie had a knack for planning exciting adventures. What would this one be like? She wondered.

The day after Uncle Hughie put his new boat on the water, he promised Katey and Will he would take them fishing on their last day of school. Sailing into Cape Cod Bay on that breezy, sun-drenched morning, he was the picture of a proud captain aboard his vessel. Whistling a merry tune, he looked like a sailor in his favorite faded blue cap with an image of a whale perched on the rim. As he steered his boat expertly to the dock, Katey watched him maneuver it, his hat tipped carelessly to one side of his head. A broad smile creased his weathered face, and beaming at them, he reached down to help them on board.

"So, are you guys ready?" Uncle Hughie asked, readjusting his cap.

"You have no idea, Uncle Hughie! I've been waiting weeks for this, counting the days when it would finally happen," said Katey. "This is *so-o-o-o* cool!" She admired the newness of the boat and the way it sparkled in the sun.

Uncle Hughie taught them how to operate the boat, pointing to the equipment and showing how each mechanism was synchronized to work together. Will was utterly fascinated with the mechanical aspects of the boat. He asked dozens of questions and stored the answers in his photographic memory.

Katey was in awe of the shininess of the boat's interior— the blue and white colors standing out against a perfect background of matching green/blue sea. She marveled at the way it gently swelled against the waves, and bent over the bow to peer at the name, *Dotty*, painted in bold, blue letters. She knew Uncle Hughie named the boat after his old bulldog, his best friend, mascot, and companion.

Speaking of the boat's namesake, the lively dog bounded over, nearly knocking Katey to the ground. Katey was doubly rewarded with a big, slobbering kiss.

"Hey, Dotty girl, do you know you're famous?" she said, giggling in between wet kisses. "Whoa, girl, you're going to knock me down again!" she exclaimed, as she playfully tousled the dog's ears. "Let's find Uncle Hughie and Will." When she caught up to them, they were discussing how to maintain and keep the boat clean and shiny.

Bored with their conversation, she ran her fingers along the seats and white interior and soon noticed a small stairway that led to the lower level. Wondering what might be down there, Katey descended the narrow stairwell. As her eyes adjusted to the dim light, she was delighted to see a cozy sleeper cabin with a desk, three built-in beds, a refrigerator, tiny kitchen area and bathroom. The dark wood walls contrasted sharply with the furniture, all of which was covered in dark blue and white. Only one small window let the light in from the outside.

"So, what do you think?" Uncle Hughie asked after they had finished, an impish smile playing at the corners of his mouth.

Katey turned to look at Uncle Hughie, her dimpled cheeks giving way to a big grin. "Uncle Hughie, it's really awesome!"

Will, who knew quite a lot about boats already, agreed. "It's definitely real cool," he said, with admiration in his voice.

"I knew you'd like my sea girl as much as I do," said Uncle Hughie, affectionately ruffling Katey's hair.

Back on the upper deck, Katey stood in front of the leather-trimmed steering wheel, gripping the black rim in her hands. "Someday, I'm going to have a boat just like this one," she said, her brow furrowed in determination. As he watched her expression, Uncle Hughie began to rumble with laughter, a twinkle of amusement appearing in deep blue eyes.

"Well, it seems to me that you're already head over heels about *Dotty*, Katey-did," Uncle Hughie said, calling her, as he always did, by the affectionate nickname he'd given her when she was a toddler. "All right now, kids," he said, stretching his arms wide around their shoulders. "School's out next week. What d' ya say about riding around on this big ol' ocean together?

"*Ye-a-ah-h-h*" said Katey and Will in unison, raising their hands to give each other a high-five.

"Tell you what: next Friday after school, we'll take a ride to a tiny blip of an island that no one knows about. No one but me, o' course! It's a place where whales and all sorts of strange-looking fish live," he promised with a wink.

Katey turned to him with a puzzled expression. "Are you sure that this island hasn't already been explored?" she asked.

"Yep, Katey-did, Green Cave Island has not been touched by human hands," he answered, giving her a look that made her wonder if he was not quite telling them everything.

Uncle Hughie enjoyed talking about his journeys all over the world. His stories were usually peppered with exciting details, and everyone he shared them with, loved to hear them. She could always tell when he was exaggerating the truth because his eyes got that funny light in them, the way he looked when he was about to tell a joke. It didn't matter, though, because she loved all of his stories and adventures.

Katey understood Uncle Hughie's passion for all ocean creatures and the immense watery home in which they lived. For as long as she could remember, she had grown up around other people's pets. When her father was not at the animal hospital where he worked, he was in his office healing the dogs, cats and other pets brought in by the townspeople. She made up her mind long ago that she wanted to be a veterinarian, like her father, and work with animals.

After that first introduction to Uncle Hughie's boat, the next few weeks dragged agonizingly for Katey. She could only think about their planned fishing excursion.

Coming out of her favorite daydream, Katey watched as the second hand of the clock ticked toward twelve. The school bell rang out a loud *clang, clang, clang* and she jumped like a runner at the starter's gun. At the same time, she felt a nudge from Janet, her friend and classmate. "Hey Katey," said Janet. "Come on, it's summer vacation—time to go home! I'm meeting Kathleen at the umbrella tree. Can you meet us there?"

"Sorry, maybe next time, Janet. Uncle Hughie is taking us fishing on his new boat," said Katey.

"Okay, later!" Janet smiled broadly, as she rushed outside to meet her friends. The anticipation of their upcoming outing in Uncle Hughie's new boat made Katey's heart swell with pleasure.

The murmur of kids' voices grew louder as they trailed past Katey's classroom. The halls of the school were soon abuzz with students talking animatedly. Everyone in her sixth grade class scrambled for the door, shouting farewell wishes to their teacher, Mrs. Fugazy. Next year Katey would be in the seventh grade and join her older brother, Will, in Barnstable Middle School. As excited as she was, Katey needed to say goodbye to her favorite teacher.

The past year was difficult for Katey and Will. After their mother died last spring, Katey's grades suffered and she became quiet and withdrawn. The terrible car accident that took her mother's life in April left Katey with a dull ache inside.

"Katey," said her teacher Mrs. Fugazy, "I hope you'll stop by and visit me in the fall and give me the scoop about the seventh grade!" Katey knew that Mrs. Fugazy really liked her.

"Oh, I will, Mrs. Fugazy . . . I promise!" Katey replied, picking up her few books and placing them in her school bag. Mrs. Fugazy reached out and turned Katey toward her so that they were facing each other.

"Now remember," she said softly, her kind eyes searching Katey's face. "I'm always here." Katey smiled and gave her a hug and then she walked toward the door. She stopped for a second, recalling that there was something she wanted to tell her about their afterschool plans.

"We're going to have the best day ever! Uncle Hughie is taking us fishing at Green Cave and he's bringing us in his new boat," said Katey, the words spilling quickly out of her mouth.

"Isn't that exciting! You certainly have a beautiful day

for a boat ride," added Mrs. Fugazy. "Have fun, but do remember to wear your life jacket…you can't be too careful," she warned. With a final wave, Katey left the classroom and was soon out of the building, scanning the crowded front lawn for her brother. Children were gathering all about, talking about their summer plans.

Katey made her way through the sea of happy faces. She found Will on the other side of the sprawling front lawn, which was sprinkled with kids of all ages and sizes. Friends were waving to each other. Some stopped at the big weeping willow tree that the children fondly called "the umbrella tree," talking excitedly about the coming summer. Although Katey usually liked to stop and talk to her friends, today was different. Uncle Hughie would already be waiting for them, Katey was sure of it.

She wondered if Will even remembered that they were going to Green Cave Island. Uncle Hughie had given the island its name after he spotted the strange green fish with eyes that seemed to want to talk to you, swimming in the surrounding inlet. The cave was the only place you could find the fish.

Katey reached Will's side. Will's baseball cap was turned backwards, barely covering thick blonde hair. He was talking to his good friend, Tim Georgi.

"Hey, Will," Katey said, as she breathlessly reached his side. "Uncle Hughie told us to meet him at one o'clock and that's in half an hour. I'm ready to get my fishing pole out and catch some of those big fish!" she added, her long auburn hair glistening like firelight in the bright sun. Neither Will nor Tim seemed to notice her and they went on talking as if she wasn't there.

Katey was in no mood to wait, noting that Will still hadn't even noticed her. She began to get impatient as she checked her watch. It was just after 12:30 p.m. He was definitely going to make them late, she thought, a warm flush of annoyance beginning to turn her cheeks pink. She was already imagining the boat majestically skimming the cool water while she baited her fishing rod. "Why are you making us late?" Katey fumed at Will.

"Hey, just a sec' Katey, be right there," he answered and turned back to Tim. Finally, when it seemed to Katey as if hours had gone by, Will gave her a thumbs-up gesture. "Hold on, I'm almost ready," Katey. Then he continued to talk to Tim, a tall boy whose unruly, dark brown hair was always flopping into his eyes.

As she waited in frustration, she wondered how Tim was able to see, let alone play baseball so well. A towering boy of six foot two, Tim did everything in slow motion except when it came to playing baseball. It was almost as if he came alive when the word baseball was mentioned.

"Hey, Will, if we don't get going, Uncle Hughie might think that we forgot," she shouted at him. "Then he'll leave without us!" she pouted, crossing her arms across her chest. When Will and Tim got together, it seemed as if she didn't even exist.

"*He-ey-y-y,* Katey," said Tim, just noticing her. "*What's up?*" Tim tossed the ball to her but she stepped out of the way, trying to get Will's attention. He bent down to retrieve the ball when she didn't pick it up, then slapped it back into his mitt. Tim paid no mind to Katey's annoyed behavior as he flipped the ball up in the air and caught it.

Losing her temper, she stood in front of Will to get his full attention and blurted out, "I'm leaving!" She was worried that Uncle Hughie would think they changed their minds. "There's no way I'm missing Green Cave Island. Uncle Hughie said we had to head out by two o'clock and look at the time," she said. With that, she turned on her heels and began to run toward their home, auburn hair streaming wildly down her back.

"Jeez, she's grouchy today," said Tim, watching her small frame get farther away. As Katey disappeared from their view, Will gave Tim a high-five and crossed over the winding path that led to the front gate.

"I better go before Uncle Hughie takes off. Katey's right, it's getting late," Will said. "Later, Tim. Hey, Katey, wait up," he shouted through cupped hands. He straightened his book bag and tried to catch up to her, but she was too far away. Will was in no hurry. Summer was here and he was going to enjoy every minute of it. Elated that school had ended, he threw his baseball cap up in the air and shouted a gleeful "whoopee!" catching it easily in his outstretched hand. He began jogging toward home. He knew Katey would probably already be there.

Will and Katey were so different from each other that it was almost comical, although they got along most of the time. He enjoyed taking things apart, building new inventions and figuring out how to make them work. That's why he was so good in math, science and anything computer related. On the other hand, Katey's absolute favorite thing to do was to play with the pets her father sometimes brought home from the animal hospital where he worked part of the week. She also liked to read and play baseball. Her passion was for all animals, and the little critters seemed to sense it. As different as they were, the one thing Will and Katey shared was their love for adventure.

CHAPTER 2

UNCLE HUGHIE

When Will finally reached their house, he saw his Dad standing on the white front porch and Katey outside playing with Gobie. Just behind her, he saw a familiar figure in a boat, cruising along in their direction. "Hey Katey," he shouted, pointing to the bay, "Look over there!"

Bright as a new penny, *Dotty* moved slowly toward them, Uncle Hughie at the helm. The sky was cloudless, the weather perfect. Sunlight bounced off its white exterior. Uncle Hughie removed his hat, waving it around in the air in greeting. It was the most beautiful sight Katey had ever seen.

"Race you to the boat, Will!" said Katey, as she scrambled to her feet. Gobie chased her, making her giggle, and reached the dock first. The boat skimmed the water easily and looked even more amazing than the last time she had seen it.

"Well now kids, what's goin' on?" said Uncle Hughie when he arrived, a huge grin lighting up his face. Merry blue eyes that sometimes winked mischievously were the most noticeable feature on his handsome, weathered face. He enjoyed any type of adventure, which was one of the reasons why Katey, Will and their friends loved him. His latest stories about "the great seas" thrilled them and they listened intently to each and every one.

"So, are we going to Green Cave Island today, Uncle Hughie?" asked Katey, as she stepped gingerly onto the boat. She bent down to pet Dotty, who was barking and wagging her stocky stump of a tail. "Well, of course, I'm already geared up for the ride," he replied. "And I have my favorite two first mates with me."

"Do you think Green Cave will have those green, silvery fish? You know, the ones you told us about that live in castles under the sea?" asked Katey.

"Now, Katey-did, you sure didn't hear about that from me, did you?" said Uncle Hughie, with a grin.

"Come on, Uncle Hughie, remember you told us last week that Green Cave Island has the most awesome fish!" said Katey. She laughed, knowing all the while that he was teasing her and just as pleased as she to take *Dotty* out on the bay.

"Okay, okay," he said, "we'll bring our sea girl out for a ride and see if we can find some of those fish. But first, I need to eat something. I'm as hungry as a whale! Besides, we should check in with your Pop."

Katey could barely hide her disappointment at another delay. But she knew Uncle Hughie had to eat. After all, he was the captain.

The wonderful aroma of cooking food drifted through the air as they walked through the door of the house. *"Mmmm,* it smells delicious in here," said Katey, standing on her tiptoes to give her father a kiss.

"So, how was your last day at school?" Dad asked, opening the refrigerator to pull out some sodas.

"It was *so-o-o-o* slow—I kept thinking about fishing with Uncle Hughie and it was hard to concentrate," Katey said, remembering how the minutes seemed to drag by all morning.

He opened the lid and stirred the steaming food on the stove. "This wonderful dish is chicken and dumplings, your

Uncle Hughie's favorite," Dad explained. "Mrs. Drummond brought it over this morning. You know how crazy she is about Uncle Hughie! It's been making my stomach rumble all day. I could even smell it from my office!"

"Okay gentlemen and mademoiselle," he said with an exaggerated French accent and a sweeping bow towards Katey, "*Everyzing weel be ready in a moment.*" Laughing, Katey said "*Merci,*" in what she thought was her best French accent, curtsied, and then began going through the cabinets and drawers to pull out dishes and silverware.

Katey set the table as Will and Uncle Hughie discussed their uncle's latest fishing expedition. Uncle Hughie was a retired U.S. Naval officer and experienced fisherman, but his biggest enjoyment since retiring was taking his boat out on small voyages across the globe. He traveled many miles on open sea to visit coastal towns and secluded islands. His passion for the ocean was obvious to many, and it was a part of his life since childhood. Katey's father often thought that to be the reason why he hadn't settled down and married.

"You should've seen the size of that beauty of a whale I saw the other day!" Uncle Hughie remarked during lunch. "It was fantastic, and glossy with a big black and white tail that fanned out," he said, opening his arms wide to show them the span of the whale's tail. "It came up pretty close to my boat, so close that I could almost touch it. There's nothing like the feeling of being on the ocean knowing I'm a visitor. I was in that whale's home, right smack in the middle of it!" he said, a light filling his eyes as he envisioned it. "If heaven is anything like that, then that was the closest I was to being there," he said, with a hearty laugh so contagious that they all joined in.

"Dad," said Katey, after they finished eating and began clearing the table, "Uncle Hughie said he would take us to Green Cave on his boat today. Can we go as soon as we're done with the dishes. *Ple-e-e-e-ase?*"

"Sure, Katey, but only if you promise to find another whale," he said, chuckling. He reached over to ruffle his daughter's hair. He was a big man, six foot three inches, and could easily wrap his long arms around Katey's tiny frame. Katey was slight, built like her mother. "Being the landlubber that I am, I know I'm missing out, while you get to see whales and fish and who knows what else," he said, his smile crinkling the corners of his eyes. "So make sure you tell me all about it when you get home."

But Katey knew her father didn't really mind staying home. Looking at him now, she was struck by how much alike he and Uncle Hughie looked, especially when they smiled or laughed. They had the same blue eyes that wrinkled in the corners in the very same spot. Their smiles lit up their faces. But the physical attributes are where the similarities between them ended. Uncle Hughie was more daring and outgoing than her father. Her father, who was four years older than Uncle Hughie, looked ten years older since her mom died, tufts of white and gray visibly peppering his light brown hair.

Katey was a lot like her mother, Alison Sarah Longley. She looked like her mother, with her long, auburn hair, dimples and green eyes with yellow specks. After the terrible accident, Katey and Will's father spiraled into a deep depression. It was only when his younger brother Hughie came around that he slowly started to get better. Uncle Hughie understood that Katey and Will needed their father now more than ever.

Katey ran upstairs to get a long-sleeved shirt for the boat ride. It could be windy and she knew it might turn cooler later. Then they said their goodbyes. "Hey, big brother," said Uncle Hughie, "I'll have these two navigators back before dark."

CHAPTER 3

THE STORM

The boat looked more inviting than ever. Katey hopped on board, with Will and Uncle Hughie just behind her. It moved gracefully through the water as the waves carried them away, a soft wind caressing their faces. Katey's heart pounded with anticipation now that they were finally on their way to Green Cave Island, where they would find their destination, the little inlet with a large cave. It got its name from the soft green moss and plant life that covered the cave entrance like heavy whiskers. Uncle Hughie had visited the inlet twice before. Katey was determined to go, ever since he told her about it.

After his last fishing trip to Green Cave Island, Uncle Hughie brought back two of the strangest-looking fish she and Will had ever seen. The fish were a foot long with vibrantly-colored scales. As different as the fish were with their silver, blue and green colors, their eyes were even more unusual. They were clear blue, not empty or glassy, and almost seemed to understand everything you said. Instead of keeping them, Uncle Hughie released them back into the bay.

"Some of the fish at Green Cave Island are one-of-a-kind. There aren't many of these types of fish in existence," he explained. "Those blue, green and silver ones with the blue eyes are called 'knowers,' and they're extremely rare."

"According to the old legends, if you're lucky enough to find a knower fish, they can lead you to an undersea kingdom, a lost land that existed thousands of years ago, now located under the ocean floor. This undersea kingdom used to be a thriving community that fell into the ocean after a terrible earthquake. Over the years, pirates and ships' captains learned about it from old ships' logs and tried to find it, but so far, no one has been able to locate it."

"Why not?" asked Katey.

"Well, some say it's because it's situated miles below the furthest tip of the Indonesian islands, in a faraway place from which no one has ever returned, even if they did manage to get there."

"Really?"

"I bet we could find it if we knew the way there. Wouldn't it be awesome to explore an undersea world?"

"Yep, it sure would, Katey-did," Uncle Hughie said, tipping his hat up as he turned to gaze thoughtfully at the horizon.

They began the ride to Green Cave Island in midafternoon, chattering happily while the boat sailed along in the breeze. Will was examining the gauges on the boat's dashboard. Katey could almost see the wheels churning in his head as he worked to understand all the gadgets and mechanisms.

Will spent much of his time inventing things. His latest creation was a small submarine with a round bubble-like window and built-in sealer to prevent water seepage. Together he, Dad and Uncle Hughie agreed to test it by submerging it in the bay. Will's submarine had taken many months to build. It was equipped with all sorts of gadgets. It was a project he began soon after his mother died and more than likely was what kept him from dwelling on things he did not want to think about.

Uncle Hughie showed them the different parts of

the boat. Will, already asking dozens of questions, was storing the answers away in his photographic memory for future use.

"What're those used for, Uncle Hughie?" Will asked him, pointing to some of the safety equipment.

"You guys are already familiar with what these flotation devices over here are for," said Uncle Hughie, pointing to the round rubber tubes with holes in the middle. "They're used in emergencies. So is the foghorn over here and the radio alarm and transmitter system." Uncle Hughie explained how red star shells provide visual distress signals during emergencies. "We won't need to use these anytime soon," he laughed.

Uncle Hughie continued. "The front of the boat is called the bow and the back is the stern. The hull is the main body of the boat," he said. "Now listen up. When I say, 'Will, meet me at starboard,' that means 'go to the right side of the boat.' The port is the left side and the propeller is the mechanism on the boat's underside that propels the boat through the water."

Fascinated, Katey and Will turned their heads to the port side. To their delight, several dolphin appeared alongside them, some playfully bobbing in the water, close enough to touch. "Those dolphins are following our boat!"

Katey exclaimed, as she watched them wiggle in and out of the water. As the boat moved toward Green Cave Island in the dark green waters, they soon lost sight of the silver-gray dolphins. A shiver of excitement ran up and down Katey's spine in anticipation of what they would find.

The sky, once clear and bright blue, was now speckled with patches of gray clouds. The clouds darkened as they moved and spread, even as the boat approached the island. Trees of all sizes made a home on the tiny island and their branches were swaying back and forth in the wind. Large rocks loomed up on one side; wild greenery and vibrant flowers dotted parts of the landscape.

"Look, Will!" said Katey, as she pointed to the trees ahead. Flying high above the trees was an eagle, circling and slowly descending lower and lower.

"It's probably found its next meal. Maybe a mouse or some other small animal," Will said, standing to get a better glimpse. As they watched, the eagle swooped down into the trees, moving in on the unsuspecting prey and then disappeared from view.

As they approached Green Cave Island, the engine slowed and Uncle Hughie maneuvered the boat toward the jetties near the beach. After tying it up carefully, the three of them hopped out. The sweet smell of honeysuckle was all about them. Abundant fruit trees and other types of trees sprinkled the landscape. They could hear the whistles and answering chirps of birds all around, making them feel relaxed and peaceful. A small cove at a nearby cave was within walking distance and they headed toward it.

They explored the island together, Uncle Hughie talking about the many types of fish that lived in the surrounding waters. They were pleased when they found brightly-colored fish of all sizes. Will pointed toward the left side of the inlet where the waters were shallower. "Hey, look over there!" he said. A big silver and green fish flashed by them in the crystal clear water. The clear gray eyes seemed to search their faces as they came toward it. They watched as it darted away to the mouth of the cave.

Katey ran after it, determined to follow its path, but the fish disappeared into the dark waters just as she reached the cave entrance. "I'll bet there are other fish like that right around this cave. Let's have a look. Maybe it was a knower!" she said, her head spinning with thoughts of a possible adventure.

"That wasn't a knower fish, Katey, but it sure looked a lot like one," said Uncle Hughie. "Knowers are green with a bit of silver and the eyes are bluish green. And they're bigger," Uncle Hughie finished, walking behind her as they reached the cave. He watched the rising water at the cave opening. Katey peeked in as far as she could. She tried to get a look inside but it was too dark to see anything beyond the first few feet.

"Can we take the boat to the other side, when we leave, Uncle Hughie?" Katey asked. "Maybe we'll find some fish over there."

"I'm not sure we can today, Katey," he said, anxiously glancing up at the darkening sky. As far as their eyes could see, the sky with its mass of clouds was turning dark gray. The gray clouds were thickening with heavy moisture. "It looks like we'll have to cut our visit short. Those clouds overhead don't seem right to me. I think a storm is brewing, although rain wasn't in the forecast for today. We'd better start heading back now."

As they walked toward the boat, the wind whipped furiously around them. The waves were bigger than when they first arrived. Katey was disappointed that they would not be able to explore more, as she was sure they would find the rare knower fish. "Oh, well," she thought aloud, "we'll come back another day, maybe next week." The next time, she knew they would venture into the cave.

"You betcha, we will, Katey-did," said Uncle Hughie. "And that's a promise!"

The rain began falling just as they reached the shore. The frothy waves splashed angrily at the jetties, pitching the boat back and forth. "You kids better put on your life jackets. The water looks pretty rough. Let's get you guys back home," Uncle Hughie said, as his eyes narrowed with worry. As he called out to Dotty, who was trailing just behind, the little dog barked, as if in agreement.

Once on the open sea, the small boat strained against choppy, powerful waves that seemed to grow even as the clouds darkened and spread overhead. Pellets of rain started to fall from angry-looking skies. Uncle Hughie was doing everything he could to keep the boat steady. As the wind blew furiously, waves pounded against the boat. The waves grew high, some almost higher than the boat.

Suddenly, Katey lurched forward as a huge wave slammed into them. She felt a knot begin in her stomach and she could almost hear her heart as it began to thump wildly. She glanced at Will, who was keeping his eyes glued on the boat's gauges, now moving crazily. Uncle Hughie began calling for help on the radio transmitter.

"This is the sports fishing boat, *Dotty*, WYS2407. Can anyone read me?" he yelled, straining to hear an answer. "We're caught in a storm, about three miles west of Barnstable, in Cape Cod Bay. Do you read me?" he said, louder now. "I repeat, this is *Dotty*, WYS2407. Mayday, Mayday! Can anyone . . ." Uncle Hughie's last words were inaudible, as a six foot wave crashed down on the teetering boat, nearly turning it over. Katey screamed and slipped down, reaching in desperation for the boat railing. Another wave spilled over onto her small frame, filling the bottom of the boat with water.

The boat was churning frantically now against the waves. They did all they could to hang on. Katey was yelling for Uncle Hughie. She could no longer see Will or Uncle Hughie. Her brain was racing frantically, as she went back and forth between releasing her hold on the railing so that she could find them and hanging on for dear life. Suddenly, sounding as if it was coming from inside a cave, she heard a voice.

"Katey!" Will shouted as loudly as he could above the howling wind, "Grab onto my life jacket and don't let go!" He found her and pulled her up, but as Katey reached out to him, another giant wave crashed into the boat's side. She slipped from his grip. Blinded by the salt water in her eyes, she desperately shouted for Uncle Hughie's help. No response. "Will! Where is he?" she cried. "Can you see him?"

"I can't see him!" said Will, his voice sounding small

against the noise from the pounding waves. He sounded so far away. Upon hearing a muffled voice, she turned toward it and was relieved to see a patch of Will's blue shirt. She began to crawl toward the blue shirt but the boat lurched again, and she lost her balance.

"Uncle Hughie, *where are you?*" she cried, in a panic now. *Why wasn't he answering?* She was just a few feet away from Will, wading through water that was now over a foot high inside the boat. She held her feet steady to stop from sliding under the water as the boat jerked up, and reached out for anything she could grab onto to stop her fall. The last thing she saw before the boat capsized was the huge curl of the mammoth wave above her head. The boat struggled against the furious waves, slowly losing its battle. Then everything went black.

CHAPTER 4

CAPTAIN SHARKLEY

W hen Katey woke up, there was a surreal calmness in the air. The moon, round and silvery-yellow, was shining overhead in a night sky bursting with stars. She was drenched, her head pounding as she tried to lift it from the wet sand. She turned her face, puzzled, and then remembered the storm. Her heart lurched when she saw Will face down on the shore, not more than twenty-five feet away. Her head was throbbing and she felt sore in every muscle in her body. As she tried to stand up, she felt a wave of dizziness come over her. Slowly, she stood and wobbled toward Will in the moonlit shadows, fearing that he was badly hurt. Katey hoped he was alive . . . *I couldn't bear it if he was . . .* she refused to let that thought enter her mind. Then she recalled the image of Uncle Hughie's boat as it sunk in the storm, just as she reached Will's side.

She knelt down beside him and shook his arm. "Will, Will! Wake up, please, Will!" she shouted, and she began to shake him harder. Slowly, Will stirred and opened his eyes. Blinking, he tried to focus on the blurry face above him. "Where are we?" he asked when he finally recognized her, his voice weak with fatigue.

"Oh, thank God you're alive!" Katey said, hugging him and laughing in relief. "Can you sit up? Are you okay?" she asked. He lifted his head and began to sit up slowly, pain shooting through his arm. His clothes and life jacket were soaked and he began to remove them. His arm was throbbing.

"I think we've washed up on the shore of an island, but I have no idea where we are," she said, anxiously looking about the beach for any sign of Uncle Hughie. She didn't recall if Uncle Hughie had put his life jacket on.

"What about Uncle Hughie?" asked Will, touching his arm where it hurt and looked around. "I don't know, Will. I don't know . . ." she trailed off, her voice beginning to quiver. A knot lodged in the middle of her throat and she could no longer speak. She squeezed her eyes shut. A rush of tears fell down her cheeks. It was as if all the sadness pent up inside from the whole year had been drained from her at this moment. As Will put his arm around her shaking shoulders, she wiped the tears from her eyes, trying not to give into her fear.

"How could this happen? Uncle Hughie is an expert. Why didn't he know about the storm?" asked Katey, almost whispering to herself.

"Katey, you know some things happen that are out of anyone's control. Uncle Hughie is always careful about checking the weather forecast," Will replied. "We'll look for him and see if he's washed up somewhere around here too. And we've got to let Dad know what happened. I don't know where we are, but we've got to try and find someone who can help us."

"But it's hard to see in the dark," said Katey, as her eyes drifted up toward the only light that shone from the silver moon overhead. "Maybe he's further down . . ." she began, her voice trailing off, as she knew in her heart that he may not have been as lucky as the two of them. Uncle Hughie had tried to get them home safely. She fought back another swell of tears, but it was no use. Hot teardrops slowly tumbled down her cheeks.

Will tightened his arm around her shoulder. He felt protective of her, ever since Mom died. Sometimes Will acted a lot older than his twelve years.

"Listen, Katey, we'll look around in the morning. We can't stay here on the beach all night, we'll have to find some kind of shelter for the night, or maybe there's a nearby town. Then we'll see how far away from home we are," Will said. "It won't do any good to look for Uncle Hughie now," he added, gently. She nodded her head in agreement and looked out at the murky water, as if she would find the answers there to her unspoken questions.

He stood up, wincing at the shooting pain in his arm as he pushed his weight off the ground. Fighting a wave of nausea, he sat down again. He raised his arm and saw the deep gash, his wet clothes still clinging to him. Katey, just noticing the wound on his arm, removed the shirt that was tied around her waist. She tried to tear off a piece of the sleeve.

"Will, I remember when Dad did this for a dog whose leg was badly injured," Katey said. "He used an old rag and wrapped it tightly around the dog's leg to help stop the bleeding." She began to examine the four-inch gash on Will's arm, grimacing as she saw blood oozing from it. Slowly and carefully, trying not to hurt him, she tied the shirt around it, knotting it tightly on one side. Will closed his eyes, pain shooting through his arm. After she finished applying the makeshift bandage, she shivered and looked around. The summer night air felt cool against her wet skin and clothes. "Do you think anyone lives around here?"

"Well, we're about to find out," he replied. Feeling lightheaded, he shook his head to clear it and then stood up.

They began to walk away from the shore, their clothes still soaked. Shivering, they continued walking for about a mile, moonlight illuminating the darkness. Their eyes adjusted to the moon's soft light and they soon came upon a small abandoned log cabin. There were no lights, nor were there any signs of people. Even so, they knocked cautiously on the door and waited for a reply. After knocking a second time and getting no response, they tried the doorknob. Slowly turning it, they swung the door open and looked around the cabin.

It was a two-room bungalow with a large, old braided rug in the middle of the floor, a beat-up-looking couch and a chair off to one side. A small, old kitchen was on the other side. Finding a light switch, they flicked it on and light from a tiny lamp spilled into the room. Against the far wall was a full-size bed, neatly made with a blanket and pillow; a brick fireplace was on the opposite wall. The rooms were dusty and cobwebs were stuck in the corners, as if no one had been there for a long, long time. Sighing tiredly, Katey slowly sank down on the chair, wondering again about Uncle Hughie and hoping with all her might that he survived the raging storm.

"We need to get some sleep tonight," Will said, as he walked around the cabin one last time, searching for a telephone. The cabin seemed safe enough.

"I bet the owner of this place used it during vacations, you know, like the small wood cabins in Chatham that people rent out for the summer. There isn't even a television or phone in sight," Will said, as he tiredly sat down on the old couch.

Suddenly, Katey felt overwhelmed by fatigue, her shoulders sore and heavy with exhaustion. She fell asleep.

Not realizing that Katey had fallen asleep, he continued talking. "I'd like to think that Uncle Hughie made it to some island shore, just as we did. If not here, then maybe somewhere else." A tired light filling his eyes, he thought about their last year. It had been a rough one for all of them. If Uncle Hughie is gone, it would be hardest on Katey. She and Uncle Hughie became very close, ever since Mom died.

Will didn't want anything to happen to Katey again. He remembered his anger after he learned about the accident. *How could she leave them? Why didn't she have her seat belt on . . . maybe it would have saved her life?* Will's anger soon dissipated and when the tears finally came one day, it seemed they would never stop. But after that day, the tears did not resurface. In its place was a strange void that was only filled when he occupied his mind with interesting activities, inventions, and computer tasks.

He watched as Katey seemed to get more and more lost inside of herself. She distanced herself from everyone. Then he and Uncle Hughie taught Katey how to help build a submarine and they told her it would soon be time to test it in the ocean. Will brought her to the baseball games and saw her slowly begin to take an interest in playing again. She always looked up to Will, but now more than ever.

His eyes heavy with exhaustion, he drifted into a deep sleep, despite the visions that filled his head.

The bright morning sun streaming through the window awakened Katey. For a moment, she forgot where she was and looked for her dog, whose usual wet greeting woke her up every morning. Then she remembered the terrible storm and Uncle Hughie's sunken boat. Discouraged at finding no sign of Uncle Hughie on the beach last night, she felt worse still when she remembered that he could be lost somewhere in the depths of the sea.

Her body felt achy but she found Will already up and about, cutting up some fruit he discovered on the shrubs behind the cabin. They were hungry and any food would taste delicious right now.

"Where did you find that pocket knife?" Katey asked him, noticing that he didn't have one before.

"I found it in one of the kitchen drawers. Thought it might come in handy," said Will. "I'm going to have to borrow it. Hopefully, these people won't miss it. I also found something else." He pulled out a strange-looking, triangular silver whistle from his pocket. Early in the morning, while exploring, he had stumbled upon it in the long grass outside the cabin. Nearly stepping on it, he noticed the silver shaft reflecting the light of the morning sun. Curious, he picked up the shiny, oddly-shaped object.

"The whistle looks and sounds real weird, but you know what happened when I blew it? A bunch of birds and two rabbits came from out of nowhere. I thought it was my imagination, but when I tried it again a few times later, the same thing happened," said Will.

"That's amazing! Katey said.

"Maybe it's *magical*," Will replied, in a teasing tone.

Katey brightened at his words and thought of something else. "Or maybe it just has the kind of sound that only animals can hear, you know, like when dogs and cats can hear certain tones that we can't?"

"Maybe, but dogs and cats don't come running when they hear this sound. I wonder who it belonged to." Will turned it over in his hand and looked at it, his face scrunched in a quizzical expression. "We'll keep it because it may be useful. And since I found it on the ground, it's finders keepers," he added, with a grin. Katey began to feel a little better. Will was so much braver than she was. Katey wished she could be as brave as him. Studying the faraway look in her eyes, Will's face softened.

"Don't worry, Katey. Once we know exactly where we are, we'll get in touch with Dad and everything will be okay."

Before they set out to look for Uncle Hughie and other signs of life on the island, Katey took a quick peek at Will's injured arm. The shirt she used as a makeshift bandage had dried to brownish red with Will's blood. "How's your arm feeling today?" she asked, gently touching the spot where the injury was hidden under the bandage.

"It feels sore and hurts a little," Will said, picking at the torn shirt around his arm, "but I think I'll manage."

"Let's go now and look around. There might be a town nearby. Then we'll find a store where we can get bandages and medicine so my arm won't get infected. I bet anything that there are people living around here. Where there's one cabin, there are others," he said.

They walked back to the shore on which they had washed up last night and searched the beach one last time for Uncle Hughie. The water seemed more peaceful today. Just as they were about to leave, something floating near the shore caught their eyes. They ran toward the drifting object.

"Look, Katey! This looks like a piece of his boat," said Will, picking it up and turning it over in his hands. As he examined it, his face became serious. "This is definitely from Uncle Hughie's boat," he said. Shiny and white, it still looked new, like it could only be part of *Dotty*. Katey reached for the object and stared. She couldn't pull her eyes away from it as she remembered how proud Uncle Hughie looked when he first showed his boat to them.

"The boat is gone. Uncle Hughie is probably gone too," she whispered. She woke up several times last night. The vivid dreams of Uncle Hughie alive, with a whale, were still fresh in her mind. She wished it were true.

"C'mon Katey," Will said, pulling her away. She let the

object fall onto the wet sand. "We've got to make our way into town, if there is one here."

Disappointed in finding no sign of Uncle Hughie, they strode toward a hill they noticed last night, the one with a large rock at its crest. "Let's head up the hill to that big rock. Maybe there's something beyond it," Katey said, and she began running.

"Wait up, Katey, let's not get separated. We don't know this place, so we'll need to stay together. There could be wild animals and who knows what else around here," Will cautioned.

When they reached the top of the hill, they were relieved to see houses scattered about a half mile below the hill in what appeared to be a medium-sized town. Beyond the houses, there were rows of stores and a harbor with boats and several small ships. Two larger ships stood out from the rest. They walked in the direction of the town.

In the center of town was a village square with all sorts of stores neatly lined around it. Two stores had the name "Centerville" displayed on the windows. The freshly baked aroma from Centerville Bakery lingered in the air just outside the store, making their mouths water. Remembering that they only ate fruit for breakfast, they went hungrily past the bakery, peeking in the window at the rows of baked breads and pastries. Drooling at the delicious sights, they wished they had some money to buy some of the rolls and sweets displayed in the window. They noticed an assortment of stores in the town square and asked the lady behind the bakery counter if there was a pharmacy in town.

"It's right across the square, nearest to the pier, sweetie," the woman said, turning her attention back to her customer.

They found the drugstore and went straight back to the pharmacist's counter.

A short gray-haired man in a white medical jacket with small horn-rimmed glasses was studying some medicinal-looking bottles. He looked up as they approached the counter. "Excuse me, Mister," Will began. "We were just wondering what you would recommend to apply to a wound."

"Well now son, what happened to your arm?" the pharmacist asked him, peering down at him through glasses perched on a long sharp nose. He looked curiously at the bloody shirt sleeve Katey had used as a makeshift bandage.

"Oh, I fell and hurt it on a sharp object on the ground," Will lied, crossing his fingers behind his back and glancing sideways at Katey. He didn't want to tell anyone what happened until they spoke to their Dad. As he studied Will's face, the pharmacist handed him a jar of disinfectant cream and a couple of bandages and told him how to apply it. "But if I were you, I'd go home and tell your parents to take you to the doctor," the pharmacist added, looking again with concern at the bloody bandage around Will's arm. "By the looks of that, you might need some stitches."

Will thanked him and asked if he could use the telephone. The pharmacist pointed to the back of the store, where the public telephone was located.

"C'mon Katey," said Will, "Let's call Dad and let him know we're in Centerville, wherever that is." Remembering to call collect, he gave the operator his home number and heard a busy signal. After five minutes, he tried again, but the line was still busy. "Let's try again a little later, Katey. The phone lines are busy. Dad is probably real worried about us," he said, a frown crossing his face as he placed the phone back in its cradle. Luckily, the pharmacist said they could pay him tomorrow for the supplies he gave them.

They went back outside and watched the boats floating in the harbor. They knew their father must be frantically searching everywhere for them. People walked by, talking about yesterday's furious storm.

"Wasn't that storm awful!" they overheard a small woman saying to a taller woman next to her who was holding a little boy's hand. The boy was wriggling, struggling to be free from his mother's grasp. "Oh yes, and because the telephone lines are still down, I went across town this morning so that I could check on my mother. I was so worried after not being able to reach her! She's quite old and lives by herself, you know," the bigger woman said, pulling the unhappy youngster alongside her.

Upon hearing the conversation of the two women, Will wondered if that was the reason why he couldn't get through when he called home. He tried his home number one more time and still heard a busy signal. "Katey, we can't reach Dad because the telephone lines are probably still down from the storm," Will explained. "Let's find out if anyone knows when the lines will be back up."

Turning the corner, they bumped into a giant of a man with a round, red nose and face and the biggest arm muscles they had ever seen. The big man had a long scar down the right side of his face and dozens of little lines and wrinkles carved through it.

"So sorry, mates. Are you okay?" he asked, reaching down to pick up Katey, who had fallen to the ground. "Where are you two going and in such a hurry?" asked the big man, eyeing them curiously with sharp brown eyes. Katey brushed herself off, and stood up. "We're trying to find out when the phone lines will be working so we can make a call," she said.

"Well, why don't you come aboard that ship across the square and use my captain's cell phone. See that big black and gray ship, the last one in the row down on the harbor?" the big man said. "If you ask for Cap'n Sharkley, I'm sure he'll let you use it. He's the smartest captain in these parts. You might find it hard to believe, but he's caught hundreds of sharks, some all by himself," the big man said. "Henshaw is my name, little mates," he added, extending a big, beefy hand to Katey and Will.

They shook the man's hand which was three times the size of Katey's. Will glanced at Katey whose eyes were as round as the moon upon hearing the big man's comments about Captain Sharkley.

"Well, thank you Mr. Henshaw," said Will, sizing up the large, ominous-looking black and gray ship with the white sails neatly lashed to their masts. There were some smaller boats docked, but none as large as the two ships at either end of the dock. As they got closer to the black and gray ship, they saw huge, blood red letters with the name, *Barking Barracuda,* painted on the bow. Feeling the little hairs on the back of their necks stand up, they almost turned back. There was something unfriendly about it. Even the name sounded sinister, thought Katey. Turning to Will, she whispered, "Will, don't you think that ship looks creepy?" Will nodded, and quietly whispered, so the big man walking in front of them couldn't hear, "That's why we'll just make the call and be on our way."

When they approached the ship, an unfriendly-looking man with one piercing steel-gray eye, and the other a strangely pale, muted color, was standing on the deck, giving orders to the crew. His expression was stony and he stood with hands behind his back looking out at the sea, as if pondering his next conquest. The large, muscular Henshaw explained to Captain Sharkley that their young visitors were coming on board to use the telephone to call home.

"The phone is down below in the cabin on the left," Captain Sharkley said, watching them with an odd expression, his mouth set in a grim line. Katey thought he looked like he didn't know how to smile. "Henshaw, show them where it is," Sharkley said, staring rudely at the two of them as they stepped aboard.

"Thank you, sir," said Will, following Henshaw down the stairs. Katey was just behind him when a sudden rush of goose bumps appeared on her arms. She felt Captain Sharkley's uncomfortable glare follow them. She almost turned back, putting her arm out to touch Will, but shook off the feeling as being silly, and stepped into place next to her brother.

After they walked down a long hallway that led to the cabins below, Henshaw pointed to a large room where they would find the cell phone. He walked back down the hall and up the staircase. Just across the hall, a lanky boy who looked about Will's age was cleaning a big cabin. A flicker of hesitation passed over his face, but he just stared at them, not speaking. Katey looked around, not seeing a cell phone or any other type of phone. The oversized room had a large, gleaming, mahogany desk, huge bed, and few other furnishings. Hanging on the far wall, its lifeless eyes staring blankly at them, was a stuffed shark, its daggerlike teeth exposed. Katey shuddered and imagined what it must have looked like when it was alive.

"Excuse me," she said to the boy, "My name is Katey. This is my brother, Will. We were going to borrow the phone that Captain Sharkley said we could use to call our Dad. But I don't see it."

"I'm Bartholomew," the boy said, his voice low, barely a whisper. "There's no phone here. The only phone on board is hidden and the captain is the only one who can get to it. You should never have come on this ship," he added, his eyes darting nervously to the top of the stairway behind him. "It was a big mistake," he continued, watching them. "If I were you, I'd leave this ship right now, while you still can." He continued to stare, his eyes boring into them, mouth set in a determined line. Katey was beginning to wonder if everyone on the ship was mean and crazy.

A sudden, jerky movement made them look up toward the stairway. It felt as if the ship was moving! Will ran up the stairs and saw that the ship was indeed beginning to move in the direction of the open sea. He desperately looked around the deck, searching for Captain Sharkley. He found him at the front of the ship. "Wait, Captain Sharkley!" Will said. "We need to get off the ship . . . we still didn't get to speak to our father and we have to get back home. He doesn't even know where we are."

Sharkley, staring fixedly at the widening dark-green sea, a strange, icy expression on his face, deliberately took his time to answer. "It's unfortunate for you, but we can't turn back . . . we're on an assignment and there's no turning around until it's done," Captain Sharkley said, his voice set in a commanding tone. He turned and looked at Will with the hardest, coldest eyes Will had ever seen. His crooked smile seemed more like a leer. "And now that you're here," the captain said, "You might as well know that we have important things to take care of first. And you'll be helping, just like the rest of the crew."

Will, stunned by what he had just heard, stared at the man in total disbelief. A surge of heat made its way from the very bottom of his stomach to his face, now flushed with anger. Trembling, he reached over to put a hand on the Captain's arm. "You can't do this!" he sputtered, his face turning redder, as a crew member looked on. "What you're doing is the same as kidnapping and you can go to jail for that!"

The captain's cruel laughter rang out, the gravelly sound echoing madly through the air. Sharkley pushed Will's arm away, and Will stumbled back. "Do you dare to threaten *me*? You'll soon find out who's the boss around here!" said Captain Sharkley.

"Whether you like it or not, you're part of this crew now. And as a member of the crew, you'll take orders from me, just like everyone else," Captain Sharkley snapped, at once dismissing him, his stony face turned once again toward the sea.

A shaking, angry Will left him to find Henshaw emerging from a cabin below. "Mr. Henshaw," Will began, but Henshaw held up a big hand and didn't let him finish.

"Sorry, mate," he said. "But when the captain gives an order, it means you do it or else face the consequences." With that, Will backed away in shock. *This can't be happening*, he thought. *This must be a bad dream.* Will shook his head as if to clear it then ran below to tell Katey what had just happened.

"I knew there was something about this ship that felt all wrong," Katey said after hearing the news. "We should never have come anywhere near it." Trembling and feeling sick with worry, Katey sat with her knees up, hugging them to her chin. "Now we won't see Dad for a long time," she said, closing her eyes.

"Don't give up hope, Katey," Will said, the angry heat returning to his face. "We'll find a way to get off this creepy ship. You just wait and see!" he said, punching his fist into the palm of his hand, his mouth set in a determined line.

CHAPTER 5

THE JOURNEY

After being at sea for six days and adjusting to a life that was very different from anything they had ever experienced, Katey and Will soon discovered that there were twenty-four crew members, including the powerfully-built first mate, Henshaw; a second mate named Big Anthony who was as large as Henshaw, but gentler by nature; a surly third mate named Tiger, all five foot four inches of him, and Bartholomew, the ship's cabin boy. They knew the crew both feared and respected Captain Sharkley.

Bartholomew, glad to have other people his age to talk to, explained that he was Sharkley's nephew and how he was forced to live with him after both his parents died. He was only six at the time his life was drastically changed. There were no other relatives who could take him, so he was forced to live under the cruel eye of his Uncle, Theodore Sharkley, who treated the boy as if he was one of the crew, working him hard and assigning him various chores throughout the day.

Knowing nothing about life on a big vessel, Bartholomew was educated on the ship by a crew member who was a former teacher. He adapted to life on board and learned everything he could about the ship, the ocean, and the islands to which they journeyed. But now, approaching his fourteenth birthday next month, Bartholomew vowed he would leave when the opportunity to escape came. He just had to find the right time.

Bartholomew had extensive knowledge about the surrounding geography and could probably steer the *Barking Barracuda* on the ocean just as well as his uncle. He had a keen distrust and revulsion of his uncle, the result of nearly eight years of living alongside a man that he thought of as a monster. Sharkley was coldhearted, ill-spirited, and selfish, and Bartholomew learned to despise him, although he hid his feelings well. He was sharply aware of Sharkley's every move, and particularly loathed Sharkley's habit of hunting sharks and whales.

Feeling sorry for Katey and Will, who unwittingly walked into a trap when they stepped aboard Sharkley's vessel, Bartholomew revealed to them his plans of escape. Katey and Will took an immediate liking to the determined, rebellious boy. They vowed that they would help him escape, if they could.

"Sharkley uses people to get what he wants," said Bartholomew. "I tried to escape once, but he nearly killed me. But this time, I'm going to get away. Anything is better than living on this ship."

Henshaw was Sharkley's right-hand man and he understood his captain better than anyone. Will quickly learned that Henshaw would be loyal to Sharkley, no matter what the situation. *That was why Henshaw was just as dangerous,* Will thought. He already knew that he and Katey would go with Bartholomew when the opportunity to escape arose.

In the meantime, Will adapted and learned everything he could about the ship. He watched as the crew busily charted a path to a nearby coastal land. He stared intently as the crew maneuvered every line, sail, and wheel that made the ship move. He learned where everything was located in every nook and cranny of the vessel. With his photographic memory, he stored away all the small details, including the crew's character traits. He learned who could be trusted and who couldn't.

Big Anthony was the most mild-mannered of the crew members, although George, the cook, who was rough on the outside, was not so tough on the inside. The scrawny little man the others called "Tiger" could be likened to a dangerous firecracker. He was loud, crude and had a quick, nasty tongue and temper to go with it. His favorite pastime was antagonizing people and trying to frighten Katey and Will, and anybody else he could. And he did it every chance he got. Will avoided Tiger as best he could and put on a stony face when he encountered him so Tiger would never see his fear. He heard lots of nasty stories about Tiger. Making people afraid is exactly what the brutal man enjoyed.

Will learned a lot from Bartholomew. He quietly observed the people around him and learned very quickly that Captain Sharkley was even more dangerous than he thought. Sharkley nearly lost his life in a struggle with a monstrous shark years ago. That experience almost severed his left leg. Although he walked with a limp after that battle, he was lucky to still have it.

Will quickly learned to listen for Captain Sharkley's

steps. The sound of his footsteps was different from anyone else's. The *click, drag, click, drag* sound his boots made as he walked across the ship's deck was a telltale sign that Sharkley was on the prowl.

Will and Katey were given chores to do on the ship, and much of the day, they were too busy to speak to each other. Will was assigned the daily job of cleaning and maintaining all three decks. He was tired by the day's end. Katey was given the job of assistant cook and server. She shared the cooking duties with George, who was the ship's cook, in the big galley that served as the kitchen.

George had long brown hair that he always wore in a ponytail. A quiet, wiry man in his midthirties—the only vivid quality in his scruffy-looking face were the intelligent, hazel-green eyes which took in everything. He was not happy to share his cooking duties with Katey. He grumbled and scowled whenever she was about. She tried to engage him in conversation, but then the scowl on his face only deepened. One day, though, when she felt especially homesick, she talked to him about her dog, Gobie, not caring anymore if he grumbled. She had enough of the *Barking Barracuda* and the grouchy crewmembers that lived on it. But George's face brightened when he heard her talk about her dog.

"Gobie always knew when we would be home from school," Katey said, as she was cleaning the carrots for the evening dinner. "She would sit by the front door, keeping watch. When she saw us coming up the walkway, her tail wagged nonstop, and Gobie's face always looked as if it had a smile on it," she said, grinning at the thought of the image. A black and brown mixed breed with long hair and big, soft brown eyes that melted her heart, she became Katey's dog almost from the first day she came into their home.

Katey didn't know if it was her imagination, but George seemed to soften after that conversation and started to pay more attention to her. Working in the big galley-size kitchen became less of a chore as the days went by. Eventually, George became her friend.

One day, when she could no longer bear the thought of losing Uncle Hughie, her mother, and not seeing her father, she began to cry uncontrollably. George, seeing her distress, asked her what was wrong.

"Sometimes, the sadness makes me feel as if a rock is wedged inside my chest," Katey said. "Other times, especially at home, I could imagine my mother at my bedside. We used to talk and laugh about all sorts of things. And lately, that sadness feels worse because I'm here and

I'm not at home. Sometimes I miss her tucking me into bed with a soft kiss."

George listened and a resolve passed across his face. He patted her head and reached in his jacket, giving her a piece of chocolate. She smiled and pocketed it to share with Will and Bartholomew.

Being out at sea made all of them tire easily, so they slept deeply at night. Sometimes, near the end of the day, Katey and Will sneaked out to the top deck with Bartholomew. Mesmerized by the beauty of the setting sun as it glinted on the softly-rising waves, they listened to the gentle lap of the water against the ship. Always keeping an eye and ear out for Captain Sharkley, who gave them little room for play, they also watched for the dolphins that swam nearby at dusk. And they feared for the whales that Sharkley was stalking. He was always on the prowl for these huge, gentle creatures.

Tiger was another story. Born in Liverpool, England, he was as fierce as he was small, and they quickly learned how he got his nickname. He was Sharkley's right-hand man and he liked to fight. He could be viciously cruel. When Tiger got into a brawl, most of his opponents backed off because he fought with intense ferocity. One time he nearly killed a man, taking his eye out for cheating him in a game.

He was in and out of jail, but the last time he was thrown in a London prison, it was for manslaughter. Out of sheer luck and an unfortunate incident that ended with a prison guard battling for his life, Tiger managed to escape from the prison. He hid in the cargo section of a ship to America and found Sharkley while searching for work.

Sharkley entrusted the fiery-tempered Tiger with responsibilities that no one else wanted, not even Henshaw. Together, Sharkley and Tiger made a frightening combination. Katey and Will stayed as far away from them as they possibly could.

One evening, however, as Katey and Will were going downstairs to their cabin, they heard a loud commotion from the ship's main cabin. The room was equipped with a pool table, small round tables, an old juke box, and a huge circular bar. Sometimes the crew gathered here to play cards, shoot pool and share a few drinks before retiring.

All at once, they heard a loud "thud" that sounded like an object hitting a wall. Curious about the cause of the noise, they turned and peered into the smoke-filled room. Suddenly, Red, a man with curly red-orange hair, landed on the floor near the doorway, only inches from Katey's feet. Stepping back, Katey muffled a surprised scream. Red was lying face down on the floor, unconscious, his swollen eye closed shut and bleeding. Tiger was laughing, a sound much like a witch's cackle. His grotesque-looking face bared ugly yellow teeth with spaces where some were missing.

"That's what you get when you try to cheat me, YOU BLOODY FOOL!" he yelled, as he grabbed the red-haired man on the floor by his shirt and cocked his fist toward the man's nose. Then he saw Katey standing in the doorway. "Why, look who's here. It's little Miss Muffet. What're you doing down here? Came to see your friend Red get knocked out?"

Will stepped in front of her and mustered up all his courage. Giving Tiger a hard look, he grabbed her by the arm. "Come on, Katey. Let's get out of here." They turned and walked back toward the cabin, loud cackles and raucous laughter following them down the hallway.

"Better watch your back. You'll get yours next!" said Tiger, yelling at them as they retreated down the stairs, his horrible laugh echoing all the way down to the tiny cabin room they shared below. Red's eye was puffy and swollen shut for days after the fight with Tiger, but he continued going about his daily chores as if nothing had happened.

They yearned to be back home, but adapted as best they could to life at sea. Katey made friends with a few of the crewmembers who were not as unpredictable as

Sharkley and Tiger. Early one evening, just as the last of the sun's rays disappeared behind the horizon, Will pulled out the odd-shaped silver whistle. It was one of those balmy summer nights with a light breeze blowing, pushing strands of Katey's hair into her face. She had finished her kitchen duties and was the only other person on the top deck. Will put the small object into his mouth and blew into it. The whistle's magical sound beckoned to the dolphins. As if held captive by a beautiful song, a few dolphins surfaced, bobbing their silver-gray heads above the water, mischievous grins on their faces. "Look, Will, they seem to be waiting for something," Katey exclaimed. "But I wonder what it is," she said, puzzled. Will was certain they would soon discover the whistle's secret. He could feel it in his bones.

CHAPTER 6

THE ESCAPE PLAN

Katey quickly learned to stay out of Sharkley's way when she sensed his foul mood. She both feared and hated his temper tantrums, which affected everyone. When a whale was sighted, his mood became even darker because he became obsessed with catching it. With Bartholomew's help, Katey and Will learned how to figure out when Sharkley's drunken episodes would start. It always happened when he withdrew into his cabin and sought to numb his brain with whiskey. He drank himself into a stupor at these times. Sometimes Sharkley would stay in his cabin for half a day after drinking the whiskey he craved. It was on those days when Katey, Will, and Bartholomew were most happy and relaxed. It was the only time they felt safe enough to talk about escaping. But of course, the tension would rise again when he was up and about.

One night after dinner, they devised the perfect escape plan after they overheard Sharkley and Henshaw talking in Sharkley's cabin. They were discussing Whale Island, a place Sharkley called a "distant land with magic whalebones that gave special powers to the people who found them." Curious to learn more about Whale Island, Katey, Will and Bartholomew quietly crept up to the door and listened as Sharkley talked about this mystical island. Bartholomew kept an eye out for Tiger and Big Anthony.

"There are precious little of these whalebones left," Sharkley was saying to Henshaw on his right. Henshaw's head was crooked to one side, as if deep in thought. "But of all the people I've known who went to the island, not one of them came back. They just disappeared and were never seen again," Sharkley growled in his gravelly voice.

He swirled the brown liquid in the glass he held in his hand. He gulped down the last half of the drink. "But, what makes you think we'll be able to get near the island, if others have never returned, Cap'n?" Henshaw asked, taking a big swig of the brown liquid from the small glass on the table.

"The waters near Whale Island are treacherous with big craggy rocks and sharks guard it, but that's not what I'm worried about," Sharkley said, his words beginning to slur. "According to this here map," he continued, pointing to a frayed yellow piece of paper on his desk, "there's a way to get past those sharks. There's another way in and I know where it is. An old witch on Green Cave Island told me how to get there, and she'll never tell another soul." he said. He turned his face up toward the light, and a devious smile played on his face. One stony black eye glinted maliciously. Henshaw smiled and nodded his head in understanding.

Katey and Will looked at each other in surprise. *What did he mean?* Katey wondered silently, as she sought to understand what she just heard.

"I didn't know anyone lived on Green Cave Island," she whispered to Will. Uncle Hughie never mentioned that anyone lived there. Green Cave Island was a small island; the same one that Uncle Hughie brought them to on the day the storm capsized his boat. Katey suddenly remembered Uncle Hughie mentioning that Green Cave Island had a lost, hidden underwater kingdom. But she thought it was make-believe, like one of his imaginative stories. Then she thought about the cave and how it looked as if it held great secrets. She wondered if it was possible that there could be a real, lost kingdom. That "old witch" Sharkley was referring to knew about it—the poor lady.

They backed away from the door, stepping quietly down the hall to Katey and Will's room. They began whispering to each other, Sharkley's comments echoing in their minds.

"Listen," Will said, his voice low so no one lurking in the hallway could hear, "We need to get our hands on Captain Sharkley's map. That map will help us get out of here and may be our only chance of escaping from this loser ship."

"I know a way," Bartholomew said, scratching his chin. He knew all of Sharkley's habits. "Before Sharkley turns in for the night, he sits at his desk and writes in a journal," said Bartholomew. "But on the nights when he has his whiskey, he always falls asleep, and is usually out cold for hours and hours."

Bartholomew remembered something else. "He's very careful about locking his door." Bartholomew knew that because he was the first one at his door in the morning when he brought Sharkley's breakfast. Sharkley never ate breakfast with the rest of the crew. Bartholomew often found him with the same clothes on from the night before, a sign that he had been drinking heavily during the night.

"If I could get at the key . . . it's the brown one he

always puts on a hook behind his door, then I could sneak in and find the map. The hard part would be making sure he doesn't suspect it's missing," Bartholomew said. "I would need to get there early, after dinner, and be sure he has plenty of whiskey to last through the night. When he's had too much, it's for sure that he won't bother to check for the key behind the door. But we'll need to be real careful because if we're caught, I'm sure he would kill us. We'll be food for the sharks." Upon hearing this, Katey screwed up her face in revulsion.

"It's a good plan," Will said, nodding his head in agreement. "But first we'll need to find out when the crew is planning to get to Whale Island. After that, we'll put our own plans into action. Let's watch Sharkley's movements until then."

"Yes," Bartholomew agreed, his mouth set in a determined line. They looked at each other, mindful of what could happen if anything went wrong. Clasping their hands, one on top of the other, they made a pact to stay together, no matter what happened.

When they arose in the morning, the sky was dark and gloomy. Overhead, gray clouds threatened rain. The wind blew hard, whistling through the air like an invisible voice. It felt like a storm was brewing. Will, going about his chores, listened for Sharkley's footsteps.

As the days went by, Sharkley grew meaner than ever. Shouting angrily at the crew, he pushed them to work harder, to the point of exhaustion. Bartholomew would meet Katey and Will in the evening, long after the captain retired. While he was in his cabin, he would reach for the whiskey which was so much a part of his miserable life.

One night, just a week after they decided to take the key that was hanging behind Sharkley's cabin door, an opportunity arose, and Bartholomew brazenly decided he would steal it. With his thoughts flying through his mind, and unable to sleep, Bartholomew tossed and turned, knowing his uncle was drinking heavily earlier. He would probably be sleeping. Bartholomew looked at the clock on the wall. It was two o'clock in the morning.

Careful not to wake any of the other crew members, he crept up to Sharkley's locked door as silently as a cat, his heart thumping wildly. With the back of his hand, he wiped the sweat beading up on his forehead. Looking carefully on either side of the darkened hallway, and not seeing anyone about, he slipped a sharp, narrow piece of metal into the keyhole of the door. Fumbling with the crude key, he listened carefully for the release of the lock and was relieved when he heard a tiny "click." As the door unlocked, he waited to hear Sharkley's steady snoring before opening it. He hoped the door didn't squeak. Beads of sweat began forming on his face as he pushed the door open. If Sharkley was awake, he thought, he would make a run for it up the stairs and hide in a secret hidden spot in the billiard room. Nobody knew about the place he had found years ago and made into his private spot when he needed to get away from Sharkley.

He adjusted his eyes to the eerie darkness. Quietly, he searched the back of the door for the key and spied it in the usual spot. He removed the key from the hook, his hands shaking, and as he did, the key slipped from his grip, landing with a loud *clunk* to the floor. *Oh, no*, thought Bartholomew, as he instinctively dove down and rolled under the desk. The key opened the secret drawer in Sharkley's desk. Bartholomew was sure that drawer held the map of Whale Island.

A movement from Sharkley's bed made Bartholomew's heart leap. "Who's there?" Sharkley asked in the darkness. Bartholomew froze in place under the desk. His mind was racing, wondering what Sharkley would do if he found him. His heart jumping crazily, he waited to hear the squeak of the bed and Sharkley's menacing figure loom above him. He tried to gather his thoughts and think of ways he could escape from Sharkley, in case he caught him. *Now, what?* Fear had turned his limbs into stone. If his uncle found him, he would be furious. He could only imagine the punishment. Bartholomew was in such a state of panic, he could not move a muscle. It seemed like hours had slipped by. Finally, when he could hear no other movement, Bartholomew's courage returned. He quietly slithered along the floor, stood up slowly and gently put the key back on the hook behind the door.

If he finds the key missing, we'll all be in big trouble, he thought as he quietly walked out the door. Turning around one last time, he strained to hear any sounds from Sharkley. Hearing only light snoring, he closed the door ever so quietly behind him. The map would have to wait for another day, he thought, heading back to the room across from Will and Katey. He looked at his watch—it was 2:45 a.m. He cursed his own lack of courage.

When he returned to the lower deck, he softly knocked on their door. Bartholomew wanted to tell them about the incident in Sharkley's room, but they were sleeping. It would have to wait until morning. Then he would tell them about his narrow escape. He was determined to get the map the next time.

The crew always kept an eye out for whales. Whaling

was against the law in many parts of the world and had been largely restricted since the mid-1900s. The International Whaling Commission was formed to protect whale populations, but Sharkley still hunted them. He fiendishly enjoyed pursuing them, and the thrill he felt from capturing them. It was a game and he liked being the hunter. But after he captured them, he sold the whale oil to black markets and countries that used the oil and other parts of the whale. Some countries manufactured the whale oil and turned it into nitroglycerin for explosives. This was the main reason why Bartholomew detested his uncle.

Days went by and still not a sign of a whale. Sharkley was not discouraged. It sometimes took weeks to spot one and he had plenty of time.

The day finally came when Katey, Will and Bartholomew could put the escape plans they had so carefully worked on into motion. Will had overheard Sharkley, Henshaw and the crew recently talking about charting a course to Whale Island. They were already on their way and the crew was planning to get there in five days. Will also learned that Whale Island is located on the outskirts of Indonesia, a faraway land he had only read about in books. It's a place with more than seventeen thousand islands that span over several thousand miles, and is situated between the continents of Southeast Asia and Australia. Sharkley recently told Henshaw that according to old legends, a lost city which existed thousands of years ago had sunk below the depths of the sea at Whale Island.

What an awesome place that would be, if it were true, Will thought. He was standing on the top deck; most of the crew was having lunch below. He took the silver whistle out of his pocket and turned it over and over in his hand. He wondered again what the whistle's connection was to the dolphins and other fish that surfaced after he blew it. Noticing Henshaw walking toward him, he quickly put it back into his pocket. "Back to work, matey. No lollygagging around here," said Henshaw, who watched him with narrowed eyes.

Will turned and went back to work. He kept the whistle in his pocket at all times, even when he was working. Hiding it from Sharkley wasn't easy but he knew he must never let him find out about it. The whistle was the key to something really big. Its special sound called to animals and even the fish in the sea. When Will blew it, fish popped their heads above the water and swam closer. Dolphins swam near the ship and looked up at him, almost as if they were trying to tell him something. "What are they thinking?" Will wondered aloud. "If only I could talk to them. Maybe they know the secrets of Whale Island." He touched the whistle that was concealed in his pocket and went down below to find Bartholomew. It was important that he speak to him tonight after the crew went to bed.

When Will finished with his chores, he searched the ship for Katey. The first place he looked was the galley. Glancing around the big kitchen galley to be sure no one was watching or listening, he spotted her at the big sink, putting pots and pans into the storage cabinets. He told her about Sharkley's plans to arrive on Whale Island in five days.

"Katey," he said, gently, "we need to build up our courage over the next couple of days." She looked at him, knowing well that they might never get home from the island with the magic whalebones. But they both realized they had to try to escape from Sharkley and the *Barking Barracuda*. They were aching to get home and see their father again. "I'm going to tell Bartholomew to meet us below in our room after dinner so that we can go over our plans. Meet me there later, too," Will whispered.

Late that night, they met when nearly everyone else on the ship was sleeping. Big Anthony and Henshaw were the only two crew members who were on active duty, steering the ship on its course to Whale Island. The rest of the crew was either asleep or in the room where most of them gathered to play billiards.

"Okay," said Will, lying face-up on his bed, his arm behind his head. "Whale Island is only a few days away. The plan is to get away early in the morning before anyone is awake and knows we're gone." His face was set in a determined line, his mood serious.

"But, Will," Katey asked, "how will we get off the ship?"

"I already have that figured out. We'll need one of the lifeboats. We'll untie the one at the back of the ship when we get closer to the island," Will replied. "I counted the boats. There are exactly four of them. We'll paddle away from the ship and stay put until it's out of sight. After that, we'll row to the island, away from the ship's course. And, since we'll be leaving in the dark, way before they get to Whale Island, the crew and captain won't realize we're missing right away," Will said. "The only thing we have to do first is get to the map. Without it, we have no chance of surviving on Whale Island. We can't possibly find our way around the island, and we won't be able to get off the island without the map."

Bartholomew knew how to handle the ship's lifeboats. The captain ordered him to help the crew untie them whenever they were hunting down a whale. As he recounted what happened the other night when he tried to remove the key from Sharkley's room, Katey and Will stared at him in awe.

"Whew!" said Katey, "That was a close call! You were pretty brave to do that. I hope it doesn't happen again. I think you'll have to be real careful next time because we're only two days away from escaping," she added, her body tingling with a mixture of excitement and apprehension. Another thought crept into her head now and she voiced it aloud. "But how will we get home from Whale Island?" It was a concern they all felt but had not wanted to think about.

"Let's not worry about that right now. We have to stay focused until we're off this ship," Will said, looking pointedly at both Katey and Bartholomew. "We'll deal with that when we're out of Sharkley's reach. Right now, I want to get far away from the *Barking Barracuda* and find Whale Island."

Nodding their heads in agreement, Katey, Will and Bartholomew knew without a doubt that now was the time to get away from the ship and the cruel clutches of Captain Theodore Sharkley.

CHAPTER 7

GEORGE

B y now, they had rehearsed over and over what each of them had to do to ensure their escape plan would work. Katey's job was to gather nonperishable food items and other supplies from the kitchen. They would fill two pillowcases with food supplies. They hoped it would last until they could find more. Katey's task was not as easy as it sounded, though. George always seemed to be hanging around the kitchen and the only time he was not about was late at night or early mornings before five o'clock.

Katey hid the first pillowcase under a big raincoat and secured it to her waist. George had his usual scowl on his face and turned to Katey with raised eyebrows, knowing she never visits the kitchen at this time. "What are you doing in the kitchen at this hour, missy?"

Katey was sure that George could see her knees trembling. She opened her mouth to speak, despite the dryness that suddenly made the words sound strange to her own ears.

"My brother and I are so-o-o-o hungry. Is it okay if I take some food to my room?" she replied, hoping he would not notice the little crackle in her voice, a dead giveaway that she was scared. But she soon regained her composure when she remembered that they would need plenty of food supplies when they reached Whale Island. They didn't know what type of plants or animals lived there, or even if water would be available.

"Well, go ahead, but make it quick. I'll be back in ten minutes to close up the kitchen," he replied.

Luckily, for Katey, she knew George liked her enough, even though he always seemed to be scowling. Despite his gruff exterior, she knew he was a goodhearted guy. She was able to make him smile more times than not. But sometimes George was disagreeable with other crew members. He put on his "mask," as Katey called it, so that the other crew members would never find out about the soft spot in his heart. He often kept his mask on and rarely let his guard down.

After George left, Katey stuffed her pockets with small items, even grabbing a can opener and finger foods. She knew he would be back at any moment, so she removed the pillowcase from her pants and filled it with bottled water and as many foods as she could without looking too suspicious. She ran up to her room and dumped everything into a second pillowcase. After tying it with a piece of string, she decided she would try the kitchen again later when George was gone. She hoped no one else would be lingering around there tonight.

Katey did not get the chance to gather any more food. There were too many crew members walking around near the kitchen and she couldn't take anything without the risk of being seen. *Oh, no*, Katey thought, *it will have to wait for another night.* Katey knew the next time would be her last chance. They would be arriving on Whale Island very soon.

But as it happened, the unexpected put Katey's plan of action on hold. The next morning, as the sun rose out of the horizon, the crew spotted a large humpback whale. It broke the water's surface, a spout of mist surrounding the large black and white body. The whale was so close that its beautiful, doleful voice could be clearly heard.

Suddenly, there was a flurry of movement from the men moving about on the first deck. Katey had just finished with the breakfast shift when she heard Captain Sharkley barking orders to the crew. They worked furiously together, lowering the boats they needed to capture the unsuspecting whale. They knew they had to get close enough for the marksman whose aim with the harpoon gun would pierce the body of the poor whale.

"Move in and get closer!" shouted Sharkley. Turning, he saw Katey and Will curiously watching the endless sea of water around them. "You two!" he bellowed, seeing them search the dark green waters for a glimpse of the whale. "Get below, NOW!"

Slowly, they began descending the stairs but eventually their curiosity returned. They snuck back up to the other side of the ship. Katey was awestruck by the beauty of the musical sounds emanating from the whale. But she was afraid for its life and secretly hoped it would escape.

The ship came within a few dozen yards of the whale as the crew lowered two boats to the water's surface. Four men each got into the boats with their gear, the marksman with the harpoon gun ready at his side. The harpoon gun was fitted with an explosive inside that would kill the whale, ensuring it would die painfully.

Then Katey saw the black and white fan of the humpback's tail gracefully lift from the water before it disappeared into the depths of the ocean. *It was almost as if the whale knew it was being chased*, Katey thought. The men in the boats rowed furiously toward the spot where they saw the tail dip under the surface. Everything got eerily quiet, as if they were in another time or place. Then, in the frenzied effort to find the whale again, the men began yelling at each other to stay ready. But just as if it knew it was in danger, the whale never surfaced again. Katey breathed a sigh of relief. This time, it seemed as if they would not get the whale.

After the excitement of the morning and suffering the captain's usual foul mood, the crew bustled about the ship, getting ready for their eminent arrival at Whale Island. In Katey's mind, the island already felt as if it had a magical quality. *My regular chores seem harder and more boring than ever*, Katey thought.

She was unable to stay focused on her tasks. She thought over and over again about how they would escape, even fantasizing about it. She made a list in her mind of all the things they had to do in the early morning hours before the rest of the crew was awake. Her heart skipped a beat when she thought about leaving.

To make matters worse, Katey noticed that George was acting peculiar. She had the feeling that his eyes were following her, watching every move she made. She wondered if he discovered that she took all that extra food from the kitchen last night. She would need to be on guard, as she did not wish to expose their secret. *If anything went wrong with the escape plans and Sharkley found out, who knows what he would do to them*, she thought. She shivered, just thinking about it.

Just then, George walked over and handed her a big bag of snack foods. "Since you and your brother seem hungrier than usual, I thought you'd want a few extra snacks for later," George said. Katey gaped at him in surprise and just managed to mutter "thank you," before he turned around and went back to cooking the lunch meal.

After dinner, Katey, Will and Bartholomew huddled together in a far corner in the big cabin to go over the chores each had for tonight. The cabin and billiard table was strangely empty. They knew the crew would not be coming in, so they talked about their plans for the morning and their upcoming arrival on Whale Island.

"The ship is arriving on Whale Island at about 5:00 a.m.," whispered Will, looking up and down the deck for anyone who might overhear them, "and the three of us will quietly get off the ship at 2:00 a.m. while it's still dark. We should be far away before anyone's noticed." Once on the lifeboat, they knew they would have to paddle to the island with their supplies. "It will take us several hours to get there," Will added, "and hopefully, Sharkley's map will point us in the right direction."

Katey hoped they would get there before any of the sharks that guarded Whale Island tried to make a meal out of them. The thought of all those sharks sent shivers of fear up and down her spine. But she knew she had to be brave, so she said nothing.

Dusk was descending quickly. Will removed the silver whistle from his pocket. Looking around quickly, Katey and Bartholomew at his side, he blew it and in minutes, its captivating sound called to the now familiar dolphins. They soon appeared, popping their heads and fins up through the surface of the water as they swam alongside the ship. Will blew it again, and they dove in and out of the water playfully, always keeping their laughing eyes fastened on Will. Katey got the strangest feeling that the dolphins were trying to tell them something important. They watched the dolphins swim away as the sun slowly descended on the western horizon, its orange and gold rays casting sparkles of light on the dark green waves.

"Will," Katey said, "I believe our dolphin friends have something to tell us. I just wish we could understand them."

"I know . . ." Will said, scratching his head thoughtfully as he looked at the retreating dolphins. "I wish I could figure out what it is. You know what though? I'll bet you anything that we'll find out soon."

Tonight was the big night, their last on the ship. They discussed each minute detail of their plans again, beginning with how to use the life raft, the supplies they would bring, to ensuring that Sharkley was out cold for the night.

"Sharkley is the main obstacle. Without that map hidden in the locked drawer of his cabin, we won't have a chance of finding our way around the island," Will said. As they finalized their escape plans, the trio put their heads together so no one creeping about could hear them. Bartholomew was beginning to feel jittery and he jumped when he heard Sharkley's voice in the distance.

"I've got to get that map tonight. But if he catches me, he'll probably throw me to the sharks," Bartholomew said, chewing on his finger nervously.

Bartholomew knew what he had to do. He was going to bring Sharkley a bottle of whiskey a little later than usual. That way they would be certain that he'd be sleeping soundly by the time they planned to leave. They agreed to meet by the life raft at 2:00 a.m.

Meanwhile, Sharkley was snapping out orders to the crew. "Get her on course! What are ya' doing down there, Red? Get up here where you're supposed to be!" When he bellowed, the men scrambled. Even Henshaw seemed unusually jumpy. He nearly got into a fistfight with Tiger, who seemed ready to ram his fist into anyone who looked at him the wrong way. Every one of the crewmates knew that this was the end of the long journey to Whale Island. Each of them also harbored the knowledge that those who ventured to this island never returned. Many of them wondered why the captain was so determined to set foot on a land that seemed fraught with danger.

Captain Sharkley had a strange look in his eyes as he steered the ship on its charted course to Whale Island. Later, in his cabin, his dark, pensive mood seemed to evaporate with each gulp of the brown liquid he drank. He examined the bottle of whiskey on his desk, turning it around and around in his hands. With each passing moment, the ticking clock seemed to sound louder. He unscrewed the bottle and poured another round of the chestnut-colored liquid into two glasses, one for himself and one for Henshaw, sitting across from him.

"Well, Henshaw," he said, his evil, black eye gleaming, "We're finally going to make our dreams come true. When we find those whalebones, we'll have the world in our hands. We'll be rich, but beyond that, we'll learn the secrets of a lost world that no one has uncovered before. According to legends, those whalebones are the key to a mysterious power." He paused and stared out the window at the vast green, foaming water that moved in perfect rhythm with the ship. Henshaw remained silent, knowing there was more.

"We'll be able to control every creature in the ocean with those whalebones. It's beyond anything you've ever imagined," Sharkley continued, his eyes glittering with an odd light. "Drink up, my friend," he added, "That old white-haired witch who gave me this map had no idea who she was dealing with. And she's gone now." At this last comment, a deep throaty sound escaped his mouth. Suddenly, he was laughing hysterically, sounding like the lunatic that he was. Henshaw's mouth soon curved into a wide grin and he joined his captain in a toast. The two of them drank, joked and laughed about the future.

Bartholomew gingerly pressed his ear against the door of Sharkley's room, straining to listen to every word. Sweat glistened on his face as he heard them talk about the whalebones, the key to some "mysterious power." He quickly moved his face away from the door. Knowing that he would have to come back later, he quietly padded down the hallway back to Katey and Will's cabin.

In the meantime, Katey continued to notice that George was acting peculiar. She felt sure he was watching her, ever since the day she filled the pillowcases with food supplies from the kitchen. Concerned, Katey left the big kitchen to find Will.

"Do you think George knows something?" Katey asked, finding him in one of their secret hiding spots on the ship. Will was talking to Bartholomew about different strategies he could use to get into Sharkley's cabin later. "Let's hope not," Will said. "George seems to be an honest guy, Katey, but we really can't trust anyone. We have to keep an eye on him and the rest of the crew." Will scrunched his face in concentration, wondering how they could get Sharkley out of the room so that Bartholomew could get the key.

"Sharkley will have a good supply of whiskey tonight. I'll make sure," said Bartholomew. "At least that will be a good start. Maybe he'll drink himself into a stupor."

"Wait a minute, I have another idea," Will said, his mind churning with new thoughts. "We can distract Sharkley by getting a whale to show up!"

"How do you get the whale to show up, Will, are you

going to wish on a star or something?" replied Bartholomew sarcastically.

"Here's the plan," said Will. "I tell Big Anthony that we saw a whale! Big Anthony believes anything you tell him. That would get Sharkley out of his cabin for a while. He would have already had a few glasses of whiskey. Then, you could go to his room and get the key while he goes to investigate on the upper deck. I'm hoping that Sharkley won't notice the missing key because his brain will already be cloudy with whiskey." Katey and Bartholomew shook their heads and agreed that it sounded like a plan. They decided to try it later.

At dinner, Katey noticed George watching them suspiciously. She fidgeted in her seat under his glare, sure that he knew something. *Did he see her with the pillowcase stuffed with food? Would he say something to Sharkley?* Katey wondered and began to worry. After the crew left the kitchen, she went about the task of cleaning up the dishes, George working alongside her. Glancing nervously at him, she mustered up all her courage to ask him the question that was on her mind all day. After all, if he knew, she would rather learn about it now, rather than later. She sat down in a chair and looked up at him. "George, what's wrong?" Katey asked. "You seem upset about something."

George looked at her, his face sad and wise at the same time, seemingly even more creased than usual. "I know what you're doing and I'm afraid you don't realize the danger you're in," he said softly. "I overheard you talking to Will and Bartholomew about escaping," he said.

"What do you mean, George?" Katey replied, a look of disbelief crossing her face.

"I haven't said a word to any of the crew. The reason why I won't say anything to Sharkley about it is because I despise the man. He'll do anything to get what he wants, no matter who he hurts along the way. Even if it means using you kids to do it," George said.

"Oh I know plenty," he continued, "but you better believe that he does too, little girl, and to top it off, he's using you to get to his precious Whale Island. There are eyes watching and ears listening everywhere on this ship. Why do you think he captured you in the first place?" George asked her. "Sharkley will use you and Will to get what he wants on Whale Island. If you succeed in finding what he's looking for, he'll take it, even if it means killing you. So, I'm coming with you."

Katey's mouth fell open and she stared at him in shock. After hesitating slightly, she told him everything. All the details about their upcoming escape, including the map they would take from Sharkley tonight. She made him promise not to tell anyone else on the ship. Of the entire crew, she knew she could trust George above anyone else, and didn't think he would betray them.

"George, this escape has to happen exactly as we planned. At the very least, Sharkley won't know the details, like when and how, even if he knows it will be happening," she said.

She left George then, reminding him to meet them at the lifeboats at the back of the ship by 2:00 a.m. sharp. Katey was confused and worried about her recent conversation with George. She had begun to have second thoughts about telling him, but now it was too late, he knew everything. *Can I really trust him?* She wondered aloud. And was he telling her the truth about Sharkley knowing about their escape plans? She had to talk to Will.

She hurried to the deck below to find him and nearly collided with Bartholomew. He was on his way out of their cabin, going over Will's plan in his mind. Will was going to tell dumb old Big Anthony that he saw a whale on the port side of the ship. In this type of situation, especially when anyone on the crew spots a whale, Big Anthony would immediately notify the captain.

"See you later, Katey," Bartholomew said, continuing to

walk toward his destination. In his mind, they would create the diversion and then when Sharkley went to the top deck to have a look, Bartholomew would enter Sharkley's room and remove the key from the wall.

"I have to do this quickly and need to be sure that Sharkley has plenty of whiskey," Bartholomew whispered to himself, as if to reassure himself that it would work as they planned. "He has to have a fuzzy brain by the time he leaves his room. Jeez, I'm talking to myself now. I think my brain is getting fuzzy!" He shook his head, as if to clear it and didn't see Katey walking quickly behind to catch up with him.

Katey stopped Bartholomew when she reached him and grabbed his arm, pulling him back toward the hallway. "Hey, what's up, Katey?" he said, wondering why she was in such a frenzy. He had never seen her so upset.

"I have to tell you and Will something important!" Katey said. "C'mon, this might mean a change in some of our plans for later." Once in their room, she explained to Will and Bartholomew that George knew about their escape plans. "George overheard us talking about getting off the ship. But, what's even more weird is that Sharkley knows about it and is even letting us escape!"

"What! How did he find out? And why would he let us

escape? asked Will. He didn't trust George. He didn't trust anyone on this ship, except for Katey and Bartholomew.

"George said that there are spies all over the ship and he knows that we plan to abandon. Sharkley has no idea when or how and George won't tell him. George doesn't trust Sharkley and wants to come with us. He thinks Sharkley is using us to get to Whale Island and to find those whalebones he wants," Katey said.

"But, Katey, I don't think we can really trust George," said Will, who was wondering about George's motives.

"Will, I've gotten to know George pretty well. He's a good, honest man, really he is. He's probably the nicest person on this ship, although he acts like he doesn't care about anyone. But I think he's okay," Katey said, confident that she made the right decision. Will knew that Katey's intuition was usually right, and she was very sure of George's sincerity.

"Okay, Katey. I trust your judgment. Let's keep the plans and tell George he's included, even though I'm still not so sure it's a good idea. But we'll know soon enough. Anyway, his experience will come in handy. There could be dangerous situations ahead of us. And he might be able to help us navigate the island safely," Will said.

Bartholomew and Will kept a close watch on Sharkley's

movements. Now that he knew about escape plan, they became even more alert. They didn't want him to learn that they would be gone in only a few hours.

Bartholomew brought an extra big bottle of whiskey to Sharkley's cabin later that evening. The captain was already on a drinking binge and seemed unaware of Bartholomew's presence. He was staring intently at a disarray of papers on his desk and Bartholomew watched him gulp down the last drop. Bartholomew's eyes fell on a yellowed piece of paper lodged under the half empty bottle of whiskey. Examining it more closely, he noticed writing marks and what appeared to be water and land masses on the yellowed paper. It was the map!

"Hey you, what're you staring at?" Sharkley said, slouching over his paperwork, his eyes glassy and words coming out slower than usual. "I need to finish some work and don't need you peering over my shoulder. Now git!"

Not wanting Sharkley to notice the excitement on his face, he coolly and quickly said good night and exited the cabin. The map was right out in the open! Bartholomew's thoughts raced. *This was the perfect time to get the key, while the map was still on his desk*, he thought. He ran back to Katey and Will's room.

Will was checking the supplies for the last time when

he heard the three-rap knock on the door, the signal that it was either Bartholomew or Katey. When he saw Bartholomew's expression, he knew something really big had happened.

"Will! Where's Katey? Sharkley is down to half the bottle now! He was sitting at his desk, drinking and staring right at the map, and it was on top of his desk!" Bartholomew said, gesturing toward Sharkley's room. "If he forgets to put it away, it will be easier to get it later." Bartholomew's mind was reeling with thoughts about ways he would get the yellowed map on Sharkley's desk.

"This means that we may have to leave the ship a little earlier than we expected to," said Will, excitedly, "especially if we can get our hands on that map sooner!"

"You go find Katey and George, and I'll go up on deck and talk to Big Anthony. When he tells Sharkley about the whale sighting, you be ready to get into Sharkley's room!"

Bartholomew left Will to search for Katey. Carefully, Will put all the supplies back in the pillowcases and tied them together with a rope. He looked at the red star shells he took from the supply room and wondered if they would ever need them. He remembered when Uncle Hughie showed him how to use them in emergencies. They never got the chance during the storm, he recalled sadly. Those days seemed so far behind and long gone. Their lives had changed so much since then. His mind snapped back to the present. Checking one last time to be sure they had everything they needed, he took a deep breath and went to find Big Anthony.

Will fingered the odd-shaped whistle in his pocket and looked out over the slowly darkening horizon. Streaky gray shadows began to appear in the dusky sky. He glanced in both directions and seeing no one about, pulled out the whistle. It had become a source of comfort during the entire journey. "If you really are magical," Will whispered softly to himself, "now is the time to bring me a whale."

He blew the whistle and the strange sound beckoned to sea creatures from near and far but could not be heard by his own ears. In what seemed like minutes, the familiar dolphins dipped their gray and white glossy heads out of the water. They seemed to smile into his face. But to Will's disappointment, no whale appeared.

A half hour ticked slowly by, and still Will waited, searching the vast ocean for a whale. Just when he was ready to turn around and go back downstairs, a beautiful sight appeared in the distance! A black and white humpback whale, one of the largest he had ever seen, burst out of the water. The huge tail made its distinctive fanning motion as it dove under. It emerged again, seeming to keep the ship in its view. Will ran to the back of the ship in search of Big Anthony.

Big Anthony was rolling up lines of rope at the stern of the ship, reeling them back into the pulleys. His big, muscled arms were expertly maneuvering the ropes. Seeing Will, he nodded his head in greeting.

"Big Anthony," said Will, "There's a huge whale on the other side of the ship. You have to come and see!" Big Anthony seemed unperturbed by this news and continued reeling in the ropes. Finally, after he rolled up the last bit of rope, he turned his face toward Will.

"Are you sure? When did you see it?" Big Anthony asked him.

"Just now, when I was on the top deck," Will replied, looking the big man squarely in the eyes.

"If you're right, the Cap'n will need to know," said Big Anthony. He turned and with long strides, made his way to the top deck. Will followed him, just steps behind.

There in the distance, the wet vapors from the whale spouted up in hundreds of droplets, rising high into the air. Big Anthony quickly went off to rouse the crew, Henshaw and the captain. A chaotic movement of bodies began to fill the ship's hull. The foghorn sounded, alerting the crew to get ready for the chase.

Five men each lowered themselves into two lifeboats and reached the water's surface. The small crew would have to work quickly, as the last bit of light in the sky was fading. Big Anthony reported the news to Sharkley. He moved as fast as his dragging leg would allow and stood on the top deck, pulling his binoculars out for a better view. When he saw the whale, he began shouting orders.

"We don't have much time," he said, his words slurring. "The light will be gone in a couple of hours. If we don't get her, you'll all pay!" he bellowed in his drunken, surly voice. If Sharkley's brain wasn't already clouded with whiskey, he would have remembered that the chances of hauling in a whale at this time of the evening were slim.

In the meantime, Bartholomew was waiting for his moment. From his hiding place down the hall, he kept his eyes glued on Sharkley's door. When he heard the horn sounding, alerting all the crew that a whale was sighted, he stood by patiently. He knew that Sharkley's eminent departure from his cabin was near. Leave it to Will, Bartholomew thought, with a grin. When Big Anthony showed up at Sharkley's door, Bartholomew knew it was his chance. He saw them leave and round the curve that led back to the staircase and the top deck.

Like a deer running from a predator, he quickly darted down the hall and entered Sharkley's room. Just as he suspected, the door was open. He pushed it open and grabbed the key on the hook behind it. Uncertainly, he walked over to the captain's desk. The map was still there!

"*Should I take the map now?*" he wondered, fear beginning to shake his confidence. If Sharkley noticed it was missing, everyone would be questioned and a whipping or worse would be the consequences. He grabbed it without thinking and hid it in his socks, putting the key back on the hook. He inched his head out of the door, and seeing no one, ran out. He quickly returned to Will and Katey's room.

On the upper deck, Katey and Will watched the men in the small boats work furiously to get closer to the enormous whale, now moving further from view. The winds picked up, creating bigger waves. The skilled oarsmen fought against the cresting waves and after an hour, they were no closer. Night was fast approaching and the coming darkness was hindering their vision, even with large flashlights.

Finally, they could see the whale no more. Crestfallen, the men knew that their fate was sealed. The captain would take it out on all of them, and many would be subject to harsh punishment. Disappointment and exhaustion filled every line in their faces as they rowed back to the ship.

Captain Sharkley's face was red, his gray/black eye bulging angrily, and a furious sneer curled at the corner of his mouth. "Big Anthony," he bellowed. "You and those good-for-nothing men who think they're sailors better get your sorry butts downstairs. Now!"

The five men shook inwardly, knowing full well the consequences of the captain's violent temper. The crew was aware that the punishment would be severe. This was the second whale that got away in just a few weeks and it was enough to bring out Sharkley's foulest temper. Weary and sore from their fight with the waves, they retired to the bottom deck. Will and Katey shuddered, not wanting to think about what would happen to those poor men.

Katey and Will walked back to their room. "George said he would meet us at the back of the ship at 2:00 a.m. as planned, Will," she said, whispering so no one could hear. When they got back to the room, an excited Bartholomew was pacing the floor. Blonde hair in disarray and blue eyes bright with feverish excitement, he blurted out the news. "I got the map," he said in a rush of words.

"*What*? But that wasn't part of the plan," said Will. "We were supposed to get the map after Sharkley fell asleep. What happens when he comes back and notices that it's missing? Did you get the key?

"I had the key in my hand. But when I saw the map right there, right in front of my eyes, I put the key back. The map was inches away from my hand and I took it! I want to get off this ship and I know you do too. We can do it now that we have the map," Bartholomew replied.

Now what to do? Sharkley was already in a foul temper and he would probably hurt the person who was caught with the map. They looked at each other for a long while, and then Will thought of something.

"We'll have to hide it in a place where he would never think to look. It's a safety precaution, in case he comes back to his cabin and notices that it's gone," Will said. "I found a radio that I was going to take with us to the island. I can open the back and hide the map in the radio. He would never think to look in there!"

Katey and Bartholomew agreed that the radio would be a safe place to hide it. Bartholomew retrieved the map from his socks, folded it up carefully and put it inside the radio. The trio hid the pillowcases behind the bed, in case anyone came snooping around their room. Then they made a promise to each other not to tell anyone where the map was, no matter what happened.

CHAPTER 8

ABANDONING SHIP

None of them could sleep, knowing that they were about to leave on a journey to a place that might well be the last bit of land they would ever see. They were terrified that Sharkley would discover the map missing. Bartholomew peeked out the door every few minutes, checking for him. Finally, an exhausted and teetering Sharkley returned to his cabin. Tense and wide awake in their beds, the trio listened for any sound coming from Sharkley's room, but heard none. The clock on the wall read 12:30 a.m. In just one and a half hours, they would be on their way to Whale Island! The next one and a half hours were the longest they would ever experience in their lives.

The quiet blanketed their room with an eerie tranquility but their minds churned with thoughts as they waited. No sounds came from Sharkley's room. Even so, they did not sleep. Now, at nearly 2:00 a.m., they silently gathered their belongings, Will putting the radio and other supplies in the pillowcases. The threesome stepped out of the cabin and tiptoed quietly toward the back of the ship. The darkness cast strange shadows in the light from the full moon. Hearts were pounding and each of them thought the others could hear it. Their movements were purposeful now and they kept watch in both the front and back of the ship for anyone who might be following. They wouldn't feel safe until they were far away from Sharkley's deadly embrace.

When they arrived at the ship's stern, George was already there, quietly untying the rope that loosened the lifeboat. He was wearing dark clothes, as were they, so as not to be seen easily. Quickly going about the chore of releasing the lifeboat, no one uttered a word. When it was finally released, it hovered in the black water just below them.

Just then, a scuffling sound burst from behind and Henshaw's big muscled arm shot out and grabbed George, knocking him to the floor.

"Where do ya' think you're goin' mate?" Henshaw asked

him, eyes flashing angrily while a mighty fist rose up in the air, ready to smash into George's face. The next thing happened so quickly that Katey gasped in surprise. George, in one deft movement kicked one foot up into Henshaw's belly. With a heavy thud, Henshaw fell to the ship's floor. George took the moment to spring up onto his feet for the next kick, but Henshaw rolled away from George and stood up. A fierce battle of fist fighting continued but George ended it with a right-fisted hard punch to Henshaw's mighty jaw. The crunch of smashed jaw bone and the loud crash of his body hitting the ship's floor was the last thing they heard as they scrambled to lower themselves into the waiting boat.

George got in first and helped Katey next, who was followed by Will and Bartholomew. Two pairs of oars were lying at the bottom, and they sat quietly in the rocking boat, watching as the ship moved away from them. As they gazed at the dark, ominous shape, it got smaller and smaller. Finally, relieved to see it fade from their view, they turned to each other and yelled a gleeful whoop of hooray!

Katey looked at George's eye, which was starting to swell and would probably turn black and blue by the morning. "Are you okay, George?" she asked. "I didn't know you could fight like that!"

"I'm fine, just a little sore," George replied. "Believe it

or not, I learned karate in my younger days. I used to enter all kinds of competitions until the sea beckoned me. Once I was out here, its beauty got under my skin and I couldn't turn back. I was addicted, as the proverbial saying goes, 'hook, line and sinker.'"

Excitedly, they hugged each other, pleased that they escaped and knowing that they narrowly missed getting caught.

"I want to shout out to the mountains and swim across the entire ocean!" Katey said, grinning from ear to ear. She couldn't and didn't care to contain her excitement at getting away from Captain Sharkley and the *Barking Barracuda*. But George wisely reminded them that Sharkley would know what happened soon enough.

"We'd better steer the boat on a different course to Whale Island. We don't want to chance meeting up with Sharkley. When he realizes you're missing, he won't be turning around. He's counting on us getting to the island safely, and if he finds us, we won't get away again," said George, grimly. Katey watched George as the lines on his face deepened in concern. She was sure he knew the ocean's secrets, and if anyone could get them to their destination, he could.

The full moon above them shone brightly like a beacon

in the night. The silvery light it cast on the water comforted them. After examining the map in the moonlight, they paddled toward Whale Island. The map showed a large mountain and cave that opened into the sea. They steered the boat south. Once they got closer, the mountain would be visible, but they knew it would not be for awhile.

The pale yellow sun peeking its head up over the horizon was the first sign of the approaching morning. It slowly made its ascent, letting them know that they were getting closer to Whale Island.

Katey, looking very serious now, was the first to bring up the topic of the sharks. "How will we get past the sharks that surround Whale Island? Henshaw and Sharkley said they guarded the island like sentinels and nobody ever got past them."

At this, Will took his whistle out of his pocket. "Maybe this will work on those sharks," Will said. George stretched out his hand to have a look at it. Examining it closely, he turned it over, noting the odd shape, then handed it back to Will.

"The only other thing we can do to avoid the sharks is to paddle all the way around the island. According to this map, there is only one way in through a secret cave where there are no sharks. We would just have to find the cave,"

Will said, pocketing the whistle.

"That must be what Sharkley meant when he told Henshaw that there was one way in. He stole the map from someone at Green Cave Island and found out where the cave was. I'm sure this map has the answer," Katey said, turning her full attention on it so she could examine it.

To pass the time, George told them a fascinating story about an underwater world and lost city that was supposed to have existed thousands of years ago, before it sunk into the depths of the sea.

"Legends say that this incredibly beautiful island was destroyed in one day after a massive earthquake, but many believe it still exists under the ocean, perhaps under the earth's crust. The crust is miles thick and is below all the oceans of the world," George said.

"According to those legends, earthquakes and floods destroyed this beautiful city, but there is a belief that there are still people alive and some type of civilization, even after all these years. These people can speak to fish and other sea creatures, just like you and I speak to each other," George added.

Katey stared at George, hanging on his words, hoping he was right. "Uncle Hughie told us there was an undersea world too, remember Will? What fun it would be to be to speak to fish!" Katey said, grinning at the thought of it. Will was skeptical.

"But how can an undersea world exist anywhere near the earth's crust? The crust of the earth would be hot and gaseous in many places and no life forms could withstand those conditions," Will said, looking doubtfully at George.

"Well, like I said," George replied, "there are many theories about this lost city and proof that it does exist, but no one is sure exactly where it is."

The sky was brightening with the early morning sun that rose higher above the horizon. Overhead, seagulls cried out to each other in search of food, a sure sign that land was near. Bartholomew, who had been paddling for over an hour, was getting weary and asked Will to take over. He handed the oars over to him and lay back to rest.

Suddenly, as the fog slowly lifted, they saw a welcome sight of scattered islands and a thicket of green trees. A big mountain rose high up above the fog and looked just like the one on the map. The islands looked so tiny from where they sat.

Pulling out the map, Will examined the yellowed paper and noticed the strange markings near a cave. "I think that this is where Sharkley is heading," he said, pointing to a spot on the map. "We have to get on the island from the opposite side. We'll have to deal with the sharks. We can't chance running into Sharkley now."

Tiring of rowing, George decided to pass the time by telling a story. He told them how he met Sharkley and recalled the fishing expedition that would be forever ingrained in the crew's mind for the rest of their lives.

George began, "Sharkley is a sailor and fisherman who is as clever as he is evil. But he cares about no one but himself."

"Many years ago, even before I met him, he was known by a great many people in different parts of the world. He was an experienced captain within the fishing community. Later, when whaling was outlawed by the United States and other countries to protect the whales, he continued to hunt them. Whaling is in this man's blood."

"When he was in Australia he nearly lost his leg to a shark, trying to capture one of the largest whales ever caught. Luckily for him, the ship's doctor was able to save his leg until they brought him to a hospital. The shark that nearly tore off that leg was a sixteen-footer. It was killed by the crew. That shark is the stuffed relic that hangs on Sharkley's cabin wall. It reminds him of that terrible day. Sharkley hates all sharks and whales and would kill them all if he could," George declared. "His fear and anger has turned him into a monster."

As they listened to the fascinating account of Sharkley's history with sharks and whales, the gentle lap of the water hitting the sides of the boat soothed and cleared their minds. As the boat neared the islands, they became watchful, and wondered what lay ahead. They steered the boat to the opposite side of the island, away from the big mountain, not wishing to take any chances of running into Sharkley. The map showed ink markings which clearly meant that he planned to get onto the island from the opening in the mountainside. They were getting closer. With each stroke of the oars, their anticipation grew.

All of a sudden, a gray shape with a distinctive fin appeared just next to the small boat. They stared at the moving object and saw another one moving in on the opposite side. "Sharks!" yelled George. "Move the oars faster and keep your hands out of the water."

They rowed as fast as their tired arms would let them as gray shadows continued to surround the boat. Here and there, the gray patches lifted and a sharp dorsal fin rose up out of the water. The sharp fins had clear white tips and moved menacingly around them.

George, eyeing the sharks all around them, moved his oars swiftly in unison with Will's strokes. "These look like silvertip sharks. The second large dorsal is white and the pectoral fins are also lined with white. Silvertips are known to be attracted to low frequency sounds and they are one of the most dangerous types of sharks," George said.

Katey was trying to stay calm, but the sight of these creatures frightened her. Within minutes they were soon surrounded by dozens of them. The sharks seemed to close in on the boat. Sweat poured down George's face, and Katey wasn't sure whether it was from the exertion of rowing or because George was as scared as she was. "Whatever you do, don't stand up or move around," warned George loudly.

As the sharks came ever closer, Will reached into his pocket and removed the whistle he had kept hidden. "The whistle! If it doesn't help us now, we're all shark food." He brought it to his lips. Suddenly, the boat was jolted by something that hit it hard. "IT'S A SHARK!" Katey screamed. Will hurriedly picked up the whistle that had slipped from his hands, and quickly blew into it as hard as he could. Surprisingly, the sharks nearest to the boat seemed to move away. The other sharks dispersed and began moving away from the boat. A few continued to swim wildly, some toward the boat but backed off when they got within a few feet.

"Hey, it worked!" said Will. "Instead of coming

closer, they moved away. I thought maybe it would calm them down. Or maybe they would act the same way the dolphins did. I thought they would look at us—maybe do something different."

Bartholomew continued to row as fast as he could move his arms, not taking any chances that they might come back. They were only about a half mile away from Whale Island. Sharks were still everywhere, although not as many came toward them. Katey watched them warily, fearing another one would ram them. A second impact could put a hole in the boat and then they would all be doomed. Will kept watch as George and Bartholomew continued to row toward the shore.

A large gray shape loomed up in the water in front of them. Katey was filled with terror. She sat frozen, her heart thumping wildly. She could not take her eyes off the huge creature and was terrified that the shark would knock them into the water this time. Will blew his whistle as hard as he could, keeping his eyes on the shark. What was *this?* The sound had a strange effect. They watched as the gray and white dorsal fin turned and made a wide circle around the boat. Other sharks were beginning to swim away from the boat, the strange, almost silent sound of the whistle penetrating their sensitive auditory systems.

Not able to breathe easily yet, Katey kept her eyes on the water. She warily looked around her. When she was sure there were no other dark, moving shapes near them, she turned her attention to the front of the boat. A most welcome sight appeared before her eyes. They were only about five hundred feet away from the island. She began to feel her body relax. No sharks followed or swam near. Laughing nervously, she sighed and sat back, relief flooding her entire body.

To their dismay, another obstacle now stood in their path. About fifty feet ahead were dozens of craggy-shaped rocks scattered at the shoreline as far as their eyes could see. The only way they could get onto the island would be by leaving the boat behind in the water. The shore seemed so close yet they all wondered how they would get there without tearing up their shoes, falling or hurting themselves on the sharp rocks. Fortunately, the crystal blue waters came up only to their waists. As George tied the boat to one of the larger rocks, they slipped out and gingerly stepped across the path of sharp rocks. They would need their shoes to traverse this mess. There were no sharks here, but these rocks could do plenty of damage.

Before venturing further, George reminded them to go slowly. "Be careful where you step. There's no reason to hurry," said George. "If you fall here, you could get hurt pretty bad." They were concentrating on getting to the shore, stepping on flat rocks so they would not lose their balance. When they finally reached the golden-white beach, they were surprised and awed by the lushness of the landscape that surrounded them. Small islands connected here and there, becoming part of the whole island. A sea of islands dotted the landscape for miles.

The first thing they noticed was that Whale Island was abundant with plants and trees the likes of which they'd never seen before. It made them wonder about the types of animals that would be living here. Impressive in their beauty, tall palms, fronds lifting gracefully in the slight breeze, sprouted all around them. The distinctive sounds of croaking frogs and whistling birds filled the air. All types of greenery, flowers, as well as an abundance of trees made a home on these islands.

When they reached the shore, Will discovered a large rock that formed a perfect seat right down the middle. His sneakers made a *squish, squish* sound with each step he took, so he pulled them off along with his socks to let them dry in the hot morning sun. Then he removed the yellowed map, wrapped in plastic, from the back of the radio and sat down to study it with George. Luckily, it had only become slightly wet, and he spread it out to let it air dry. As they studied it, they were curious about the various markings. There were two circles, a star and a spot that marked an entrance to a cave.

"This is the very thing that Sharkley is looking for," said George, pointing to the marked spot on the map. "According to the map, the cave is just on the other side of this mountain and this is no small mountain. We still have a lot of walking to do. But there's no other way," George decided, putting the map down. They collected their things and set out toward their destination cave.

"There's one other thing we have to remember," George added, looking pointedly at each of them as if to make sure his words would be embedded in their brains. "We must stick together. We don't know what dangers lay ahead of us."

"And remember what Sharkley told Henshaw," Will chimed in. "No one has ever returned from Whale Island alive and there has to be a reason why. A reason that someone or something wants to keep a secret."

Katey and Bartholomew looked at him, then turned to George with hands and arms outstretched. The four clasped hands, one on top of the other. They vowed they would stay together for their safety. Then they set out on the long journey to the cavernous mountain.

CHAPTER 9

THE RAIN FOREST

The sun was yellow orange in a deep blue sky. They were in high spirits and checked their surroundings curiously, noticing the profusion of shrubs and flowers all around them. Colorful, flowering plants of all sizes and shapes with magnificently displayed blooms were spread throughout. After they left the sand dunes near the shore, they came upon wide, grassy plains dotted with a plethora of trees. In the distance, they could see a dense forest.

As she rolled up her pants, Katey wiped her face, which was beginning to turn pink from the sun. The island climate was humid and tropical. Will stopped for a minute and took out the map to examine it. "It looks like we'll have to go through that forest before we can get near the mountain," he said.

"What do you think lives in the forest here?" asked Katey, who was imagining large, ferocious animals lurking about.

"Well, most tropical island inhabitants include the usual: monkeys, apes, birds, and other small animals. I don't think we'll have to worry about any lions, tigers or bears, if that's what you're worried about, Katey," George said reassuringly. "But, just the same, let's stay together."

"And, don't forget," Will pointed out, "I have the whistle. It might protect and even help us. Most animals seem to like its sound, except for sharks."

"Don't worry, Katey," added George, patting his side where he hid a weapon. "I brought along a knife my father gave me years ago. I've kept it close to me ever since. I never did trust Sharkley, so I kept it hidden on the *Barking Barracuda*. I stored it under my mattress at night. It was never far." Katey took some comfort in his words. Then she ran to catch up to Bartholomew. He stood hunched over a small shape that looked like an animal.

To Katey's delight, a small lizard-like critter skittered across her path. She ran to snatch it up before it could scoot away. The little green and brown creature was quick, though. As soon as she got close, it would take off in a quick burst and move on to another spot in the grass. She ran after it but stopped again a few feet away. "You won't slip away this time, said Katey to the tiny creature. She crept up to it slowly and stretched out her hand. This time, she was too fast for him. She grabbed his tail and shouted with glee at her good fortune.

"Gotcha, little guy!" She dangled him by the tail and then cradled him in her palm. "I'm going to call you 'Rex,'" she said. She marveled at how much he looked like a miniature Tyrannosaurus Rex dinosaur, except that he scrambled on all fours. Not only was he much less frightening because of his size, she thought he was a lot cuter.

Bartholomew laughed at the sight of Katey, dangling her prize by its tail. She scooped the lizard up in her other hand and was amazed that it just fit in her palm, except for its tail. It squirmed a little, but Katey held on. Then it relaxed, and when she opened her palm, it stayed put.

"I tried to get my hands on one of those little lizards too, but it was too fast for me," Bartholomew said, laughing.

As Will and George caught up with them, Will reached for the little creature resting in Katey's palm. "He's a cute little fella, isn't he?" said Will. Then he remembered that there were probably many types of animals on the island. He knew it could be dangerous running off in unfamiliar surroundings.

"I wouldn't go wandering off by yourself when we get to the forest, Katey. There's probably a lot more critters in there, and some might not be too friendly," Will said.

George agreed. "Will's right, Katey. This is an island that could be dangerous. We might find other types of animals. Maybe even some we've never seen before," he said. "We just have to be cautious and remember to stay together," he added, knitting his brows together as he turned his thoughts to the forest just ahead.

George picked up the pillowcases that held the supplies and handed one to Bartholomew. They were taking turns carrying them. Then they all trudged off in the direction of the forest. Katey was convinced that the forest seemed a lot less friendly than before.

The climb became steeper as they continued to walk up a small grassy hill that was sprouting with small, low-growing flowers. Above them, they could hear the sounds of strange bird whistles and rustlings from the branches overhead. They were fascinated by the unfamiliar sounds. A colorful bird of red, blue, green and yellow surprised them when it flew from the tree next to them into a nearby tree.

The tree gave off a wonderful fragrance of nuts and wood.

"Look, there's a parrot," said Katey, watching the bird with the colorful plumes fly into the higher tree. Several other parrots were sitting in the branches above her. Her eyes turned downward to a nearby tree trunk where a small group of what looked like miniature deer were milling about. The little deer, seeing them approach and sensing danger, darted quickly away into the safety of the thick the forest beyond.

"Oh, how beautiful! I have never seen such tiny deer before. They looked like babies," said Katey. This place was like an animal paradise to her. Forgetting about what Will said about the unpredictable dangers of the forest, she became more curious with each step. The flowers were most unusual with magnificent colors and sizes. Still holding Rex, she stopped to gaze at the biggest flower she had ever seen in her life.

Catching up to her, Bartholomew's mouth fell open when he saw the huge petals displayed on the unusual red flower before his eyes. "Wow!" exclaimed Bartholomew, his mouth still agape. "That has got to be a monster flower! I have never seen one that big before."

As they looked around, they noticed there were several of these flowers scattered about. As pretty as they were on the outside, when one got too close, there was an unpleasant odor of rotten meat that came from them. The flowers, with their dark red petals, spanned at least two feet in width.

"What type of flower do you think this is?" Katey asked no one in particular, her eyes widening into two large circles. George looked at the giant flower and immediately knew what it was.

"I've seen these flowers before on other remote islands. But they're very rare and they live on only a few islands in the world," George said. "This is the Rafflesia Arnoldi, the largest flower in the world. Its favorite food is bugs and flies. The plant attracts its prey with a pungent smell, much like meat that's gone bad, and when its victims least expect it, boom! It closes in on the flies and other bugs, and they become a tasty meal. It's very rare and is threatened to become extinct."

Katey screwed up her face at the thought of eating bugs. "That doesn't sound too tasty. But it reminds me that I'm so hungry!" Katey exclaimed. They hadn't eaten in a long time and their stomachs were telling them they had better have something soon. They found a small clearing with rock outcrops where they could sit down and eat some of the food from the supplies Katey packed. She pulled out a can opener from the pillowcase and opened two cans of beans.

They feasted on beans, bread and a couple of snack bars.

"This isn't exactly my idea of a great lunch, but it tastes wonderful anyway," Katey commented. The others agreed and ate hungrily, knowing they would have to conserve their food supply until they found more they could eat on the island. They twisted open the tops of the water bottles and drank half, saving the other half for later. Their supplies were limited and it was clear they would have to replenish them soon.

Chatting easily while they finished the last bits of their meal, they gathered up the supplies they would need later. Setting out for the forest once again, Will began whistling a tune. The catchy tune was contagious and soon they all joined in, eventually breaking out in song and laughing at each other. After awhile, they became quiet and continued walking. Will noticed more odd plants and insects. "Well I can tell you one thing," he quipped, "We definitely don't have plants or bugs like this at home!"

The sweltering midday heat was stifling. The heavy foliage growing throughout the forest made the air seem thicker. Katey wished they could be back at the shore so she could jump in the water. This island was near the equator and the humidity made it feel like 110 degrees. The forest felt like a greenhouse during summer.

A loud rustling noise made them turn toward the sound, and they looked up in time to see a furry brown chimpanzee leap from one tree branch to another. Katey was mesmerized by the family of playful chimps that followed, leaping from branch to branch, and entertaining them with their wild antics. A patch of orange hair near the low branches of a nearby tree caught Will's attention. He saw the longhaired creature sit solemnly down on the branch. Suddenly, it sprang down and hung by one arm, dangling the second long, orange arm at its side. "It's an orangutan!" said Will. "It's the first time I've seen one up close."

"That looks like a young one," noticed George. "We better move on, because the mother might be around, and she won't be as cute, especially if she finds us near her baby."

They knew George was right, but their curiosity would not allow them to leave quickly. Although Will knew that orangutans could be aggressive, they were not known to attack humans. Still, they could not take any chances and soon moved on. After leaving the thickness of the forest, the air seemed to flow better and they breathed a little easier. They took a long drink of the now warm bottled water, thirsty from the heat of the day.

A big mountain loomed closer and they knew this was the one they were searching for—*their* mountain.

Next to it, on one side, was a stretch of three smaller, oddly-shaped mountains. They learned later that these creviced mountains covered with lumps and bumps were actually volcanoes. Some of them were still active. On the other side of the mountain was a cave, clearly the one marked on the map. They still wondered about the meaning of the star and two circles scribbled on the map right next to the mountain.

They could see blue from the water in the distance. Just beyond the mountain was a lagoon and they continued to walk toward it. Even from where they were, the water looked inviting in the heat of the day.

In another expansive, rocky clearing that led to the dense mountain forest, they found much of the same types of plant life as in the place where Katey discovered Rex. She looked at her hand and knew she had to get him up to the high grassy areas he was familiar with. He needed to find food and grow with his own kind. She gingerly set him down onto a patch of grass much like the grassy area where she caught him.

"Goodbye, Rex," she said, sadly. "You need to stay with your own natural friends." With that, Rex sat rigidly in the grass, staring with unmoving eyes in the same spot where she placed him. Then, with a flick of his small tongue, he darted away in a sudden burst of energy and was gone from sight.

They were soon at the foot of the mountain, surrounded by the picturesque lagoon. It looked even more inviting than the Cape Cod Bay back home. Nothing looked as cool, refreshing or as inviting at this moment. They were nearly there. From the corner of his eye, Will saw a sudden movement. It came from the small cave entrance on their left side. Frozen with shock at what he thought he just saw, he recovered quickly. He was the first to spring into action.

"Come on, we've got to run! Don't look around, just run!" Will said, and he sprinted toward the first tree he could find and climbed up as fast as he could. He reached a high, thick branch and looked down as Katey and the others followed him, Bartholomew in the rear. "Hurry, hurry," he said, gesturing with his arm to make them move faster. As they continued to climb, Katey chanced a look beneath her. She could hardly believe her eyes at the creature that was gaining on Bartholomew.

He was the last one to climb up the tree but Bartholomew was not quick enough to escape entirely. The largest, brownish-gray colored lizard he ever saw opened his wide jaws and nearly took off a piece of his foot as he continued to struggle upwards. The fierce creature looked to be about twenty-five feet long. Will yelled again, "Hurry Up! You've got to move faster!" Bartholomew, whose leg was now only inches from the monster, was not fast enough. All he could see as he strained to see below him, was a wide, gaping mouth straining to get a piece of his leg.

"Help me, he's gaining on me!" Bartholomew cried, not stopping to look down but imagining he could feel the creature's breath on his leg.

Then they heard a rapid series of movements on the ground that sounded like a muffled machine gun. It was coming from another giant lizard that arrived on the scene, and he too, was trying to climb up the tree. The first one lunged at Bartholomew who scrambled to reach the higher branches.

Reaching with his arm down, George grabbed at Bartholomew's arm as hard as he could and hoisted Bartholomew into the tree branch closest to him. The huge animal opened his great jaws and snapped down. At the very same time, Bartholomew lifted his legs up and scrambled in a sideways motion on the wide branch. He narrowly escaped losing part of his leg to the creature below. As his heart continued to race, he felt relief flood over him and wiped at the sweat pouring down his face, now flushed beet red.

They stared down from the branches where they perched, still in shock. The brown and gray creatures looked like a combination of a dinosaur and a large lizard, with cold, yellow-brown eyes that seemed to bore into them, and a long, yellow forked tongue that continually darted in and out. It seemed to be testing the air with its tongue, as if trying to taste it. Then, as suddenly as it appeared, it just as quickly lost interest and turned back toward the small cave entrance from which it came. The larger of the two, lumbering along, disappeared into the cave just behind the smaller lizard.

"What in the world was that?" asked Katey, still shaking from the encounter and watching as the strange creatures retreated into the cave. She refused to get out of the tree until she was quite sure they would not be returning.

"Those are Komodo dragons," replied George. His voice seemed to come from far away. "I've seen one or two on other nearby islands in these parts of the world, but never this close. They only live in tropical islands, right around this area. The Komodo dragon is thought to be a descendant of the dinosaur. Not only do they have powerful jaws and claws, they can grow as big as twelve feet. They live in these parts, and there are only about two thousand left in the world, although they have survived for millions of years."

"Wait," said Will. "I remember learning about the Komodo dragon in school. We had to do reports on nearly-extinct animals and the Komodo dragon was one of them."

"The dragon moves fast and those loud foot movements, like the one we heard before it tried to take a bite out of Bartholomew's leg, are a sign that it's ready to attack. They are extremely aggressive and nothing will stop them once they attack. And they are carnivorous and can eat large animals. They like to eat small deer and wild boar, and will eat younger Komodo dragons, even their own offspring. Young dragons survive adults by hiding and living in trees. The adults prefer to spend their time on the ground."

"Not very good parents are they?" said Bartholomew, still panting with exertion, his face flushed. Katey, laughing at Bartholomew's comment, was impressed by George's knowledge. She looked around, up, and down to be sure there were no young Komodos sharing the tree with them.

"Well, you both know a lot about the Komodo dragon. As for me, I didn't know that dragons still existed. When I think about dragons, I see giant green monsters with wings, a long tail and hot, fiery breath," said Katey, remembering the fantasy books she liked to read at home. She thought that dragons were purely imaginary inventions from the days of King Arthur. Even though these did not breathe fire, they still looked scary. In an afterthought, she checked the tree again, just in case there were any small dragons waiting to pounce on them from branches above. Seeing none, she relaxed a bit.

Bartholomew reached down and examined his foot, the one that the dragon was after. "Listen you guys, next time let me go up the tree first when you see any kind of large animal chasing us," Bartholomew said. At that they all had a good laugh. Bartholomew's ankle looked red and puffy. A long red cut was still bleeding in the place where it caught a tree branch in his frenzy to get away from the dragon.

"Now what are we to do?" Katey asked, looking at Will and George for an answer. "We can't sit up here forever, but I'm not ready to get down yet. What if there are more of them hiding in the cave? Or worse, what if there are hundreds of them, like the sharks?"

George chuckled at the expression on Katey's face. She looked down, wondering if there were more of these Komodo dragons lurking around, and she bit her lip nervously.

"You have a good point there, Katey. But, it's getting

late and we can't be sitting in this tree all night. I say that we head for the mountain before it gets dark and find some kind of shelter for the night. We can set up camp there and stay until the morning."

Just then Will remembered his whistle and removed it from his pocket. "Look at that!" he said, tossing it up and catching it in his hand. I forgot about it."

"What good are you, Will," asked Bartholomew, still examining his ankle. "I could have died if that beast bit off my foot!"

At this, they laughed again, relieved that all of them were safe.

"But really, I wonder what would have happened if the dragons heard it? Will asked. "Remember how the sharks went away when I blew it, but the dolphins and other animals came closer? This whistle is still a mystery; that's for sure. The mysterious magic whistle." Then he returned it to his pocket and they began their descent to the ground below.

As they slowly climbed down from the tree, they were glad that it provided safety from the dragons. They were even more cautious now after their experience, and hoped they would not find another one crossing their path. Will fingered his whistle nervously and George put his knife in his belt buckle, right at the pocket of his pants where he could grab it quickly, if needed.

Katey checked Bartholomew's leg, wetting a piece of her sleeve with the water in the bottle to pat it clean.

George took a look at it too. "Let's see if we can find some aloe leaves in the absence of medicine," said George. "Aloe will reduce the swelling and help the healing process along."

They began walking toward the mountain, on high alert to any unusual sounds. All of a sudden, they realized that they were actually on the mountain and climbing its lush landscape. It was bountiful with natural beauty. They heard the distinct sound of other animals and knew they would have to be watchful. They had already seen tiny lizards, small deer, chimps, orangutans, and dragons. Katey hoped they would never see another Komodo dragon.

As they began climbing the steeper parts of the mountain, a clump of birds flew in a pattern just above them, and Katey watched, amazed at their brilliant colors. Will didn't think they looked like birds at all and was trying to figure out why, when one of them came down close in a scooping motion. He realized then that these were not birds. Most of them had a wingspan of almost a foot and iridescent blue-black with green markings on their wings.

"Those are butterflies! The biggest butterflies I've ever

seen!" cried Katey, shielding her hand over her eyes from the late afternoon sun.

They watched, mesmerized, as the huge butterflies, gently flapping and fluttering their enormous wings, put on a graceful show—a dance that was enchanting. Dipping high and low in graceful motion, they seemed just as curious about the humans as they were about the butterflies. Then, they took flight high up toward the sky until the last one disappeared from sight.

"Wow," said Katey, a dreamlike expression on her face; "that was so beautiful. I wish they would have stayed."

"That was awesome!" agreed Bartholomew, his eyes lit with excitement and jaw still open. "Those were some amazing butterflies. You know, so far, we've seen huge butterflies and humongous lizards. I really hope that doesn't mean that we'll find only monster-size animals around here. This place has the biggest and the smallest creatures I've ever seen. Nothing in between." Katey giggled at his comments and Will smacked him on the back and laughed.

The trek through the mountain became steeper. Soon, they came upon a cave carved into the mountain's side. Interesting rocks sprawled around it and a huge flat rock jutted out above it. "This cave looks pretty big," said Will.

"Yes, and dark," Katey whispered, sure that something might be hiding inside.

George bent down and picked up a large tree branch. "This is a good size for a torch. A torch will help us find our way around the cave and keep animals and other dangerous creatures away. I also have two flashlights, but I think we should save them for when it's absolutely necessary," said George, reaching into his pocket to show them.

"If this cave cuts through the mountain, we'll reach the other side a lot quicker. But remember, ALL OF YOU," George emphasized, "We need to stick together. For now, I think we should stay here and camp out for the night. This would be a good campsite. It's sheltered by that large rock overhang."

"I don't know about you," said Bartholomew, "but I'm starving." And with that, he dropped the pillowcase to the ground and sat down. Exhausted and hungry, they opened the supplies and found canned tuna fish, a loaf of bread and snacks. They opened the bottled water and this time drank the entire bottle to quench their voracious thirst.

"We'll need to find water somewhere. We're running out," Bartholomew said, looking at his depleted water supply. Weary, they sat down under the shelter of the rock overhang and ate the food they brought. Their supplies were getting low. They would have to find fruit and other food soon to sustain them. They needed all the energy they could get for the tough days ahead.

The sun was setting, leaving behind orange and yellow streaks of color in the sky, some parts turning grayish blue. George gathered wood for a fire to help warm them through the night, and to keep away stray animals. Katey dreamed about Uncle Hughie in a beautiful land with dolphins and whales swimming among the people who lived there. She slept long and soundly throughout the night.

CHAPTER 10

THE BONES OF WHALE ISLAND

After a breakfast of blackberries that Will found on nearby bushes, they ventured further into the cave. They opened one of the two loaves of bread and hungrily devoured it. They were running low on water and Will knew they would soon have to find fresh water. Although it was bright outside, inside the cave, Bartholomew turned on the flashlight and George lit a torch with some of the wood they found.

The cave was chilly and rock formations jutted out from all sides of its walls like thick tentacles, trying to catch unwary visitors. As they walked along, the cave widened.

Formations of stalagmites and stalactites in intense colors sprang up and down from floor to ceiling in massive growths. It was an impressive sight. Some of the rounded mounds of stalagmites reached up to heights that were even taller than George. There were some odd-shaped ones which looked like broomsticks with shiny bits of crystallized material growing on them. The ground was dry here, but after walking for some time, the foursome found it became moist. Large formations of unusual rocks with jagged edges and white to tan colors brightened the cave.

As George walked over to examine one of the stalagmites, his knife slipped to the ground. It made a startlingly loud noise that echoed and woke flying creatures hiding in crevices. "BATS!" shrieked Katey, watching them swirl around in an angry cloud of black shapes.

Hundreds of bats flew around them wildly, squeaking loudly, apparently awakened from slumber by the deafening noise. After what seemed like hours, but in reality was just a few minutes, the bats returned to the crevices in which they all but disappeared, gathering in clumps together.

Katey was still holding tightly onto Will's arm. She was fearful that the bats would bump into them and stick in her hair, as she heard they could do. She relaxed her hold on him after the bats returned to their hiding spots.

A few of them remained, scattered in the air above them, as if confused.

George picked up the knife that caused all the trouble. "There are probably many types of marine and land animal life here, so we should tread lightly. We don't want to disturb any of the creatures that make a home here," George warned.

"I think George is right," Will added, looking around him cautiously. "Let's move along as quietly as we can."

The cave sloped steeply as they descended into a chamber that was aglow with glittering, magnificent concretions. They stared, mesmerized, at the sparkling bits of substance that lit up the cavern and filled the room with radiant light. Sitting on a rock to rest, they looked around at the beauty surrounding them. Never in their wildest dreams would they have ever believed that a cave could produce natural light such as this. It looked as if they were outside on a bright, sunny day. After awhile, they continued, progressing slowly along a rocky path and soon came upon small animal bones that were scattered on the cave floor.

"This cave could be a home to larger animals," George said, after examining the bones. Realizing that larger animals could be living in the cave, they proceeded cautiously.

They walked for what seemed like hours until they

heard the trickling sound of running water. It was directly ahead of them. A steady stream of water was flowing slowly down one side of the massive rocks. George tasted it and immediately spat out the bitter-tasting fluid. "We've got to find drinking water somewhere on this island," he said, looking at the dwindling bag of supplies. A faint bit of light appeared in the distance. "Look ahead. That must be the way out of this cave," he said, seeing the light in the distance. He pointed to the distant light filtering into the cave. Katey whooped with delight at seeing daylight.

Their spirits soared as they realized they would soon be outside again. As they walked, rock formations with huge crevice-like openings surrounded them on all sides. The cave widened again and they began to feel as if they were walking down a hill. As they continued to walk further down, water gathered in a pool at their feet. They hesitated before beginning to walk through it, not sure how deep the water was.

There was no getting around the water before them, as the cave narrowed and there was no other place to walk. Katey was beginning to wonder about the sharks again, and if they would be in the water. It looked menacing and she kept her eyes wide open for shark sightings. She looked for gray patches and raised dorsal fins, a sure sign that sharks were about, and felt all her muscles tense.

George was still holding his torch up high, and he warily watched the water too.

The huge crevices in the rocks lining the walls made it too dangerous to try to walk along the rocks. The water was now nearly hip level and was getting deeper as they moved along. They heard the splashing of water against rocks, which meant that they would soon be leaving the cave. Bartholomew tied one of the supply pillowcases around his waist as the water weighed the supplies down, making it increasingly difficult to carry. Will did the same with the other pillowcase. When the water came up to shoulder level, they knew they would have to start swimming. The light from the end of the cave opening was closer.

"I don't swim very well," said Katey, looking around at the deepening water. "Don't worry, Katey," said Will. "Just hang onto me, if you find yourself slipping. We're almost at the end now."

Paddling through the water furiously, they soon reached the opening. On the other side, turquoise-blue water flowed into the cave opening. Foamy waves lapped against the rocks that shaped the cave entrance. On their right side was a sandy alcove and the shoreline. Directly in front of them, they were delighted to see a lovely lagoon, with large rocks of all shapes and sizes adorning its landscape.

The rocks made a pretty landscape in the water, and a wide opening through two large rock formations that almost formed a circle, led out to the sea.

They swam to the sandy area at the shore of the lagoon. Dragging themselves onto the white sand speckled with gold, they sat, relieved to have the ground beneath them again. Beyond the sandy beach, they could see hills scattered with trees and other growth. Another cave entrance could be seen further down on the opposite side of the lagoon directly across from the cave they had just left.

Will and George retrieved the map from Will's pocket. The wet plastic bag around it had kept the map dry and now he examined it. They realized that the spot on which they were standing was the one Sharkley had marked in black ink on the map. Wandering across the sandy shoreline, Katey looked back at the cave entrance and noticed long, thin grayish objects partially embedded in sand. Walking over to see what the unusual objects were, she pulled and removed them from the sand. She looked at them curiously. "Hey, everyone, look what I found," she said, turning one of them around in her hand to figure out what it was.

"Where did you find this, Katey? George asked her. "There are some more of them scattered along the beach," Katey replied, running to the spot where she found the strange-looking objects. She bent over and picked up some of the other ones scattered about. George and Will bent over and collected about a dozen of them. There were more than one hundred of the long, bony strips on the shoreline and near the cave entrance. George examined them carefully and realized what they were.

"These are whalebones. They actually come from the mouth of a certain type of whale. This is 'baleen' and it comes from humpback whales. These types of whales don't have teeth, so they use their baleen to strain food through their mouths," George told them, flipping the strange-looking bone around in his hands as he spoke.

"Baleen is strong and flexible and was considered valuable during the whaling days. It produced many things, including fishing rods, umbrellas, carriage springs, and even ladies' corsets."

What are corsets?" Katey asked.

"Corsets were supposedly a necessary part of a woman's attire back in the 19th century. They wore them in their dresses to help shape their figures," George explained. "Although, I don't know how in the world they could breathe in them!"

Katey and Will learned about the history of whaling in school. In the 19th century, it was a booming industry in the U.S. and other parts of the world. Bartholomew knew a lot about whaling too, probably as much as George.

"Although in the last few decades, whaling has been banned in many parts of the world to protect the whales, Sharkley still continued to hunt them," explained George. "He hunted them for sport and for their body parts. Certain parts of a whale's body are valuable in other countries and are sold for large sums of money. These whale parts are used to manufacture different types of products, which are then sold to people who need them."

Listening to George's explanation about how whale parts are used, Bartholomew became increasingly agitated.

"I know exactly what baleen is," Bartholomew said, knitting his brows together. He remembered vividly the way Sharkley killed the humpbacks and his face became angry. "Sharkley kills the whales and saves the baleen and oil to sell to other countries. He killed them for that and other things," Bartholomew explained. "I remember how he treated those whales. I would've liked him to feel how those whales felt when he hunted them down," Bartholomew said, his face red as he recalled those whales and the slow, torturous way they died after they were captured. The marksman with the harpoon was the eventual doom of the whale. As the whale tired from trying to escape, it also lost a great deal of blood and eventually died.

George knew how much Bartholomew despised his uncle. He could barely tear his eyes away from the crew when they captured a whale. He often wondered if they realized their cruelty to the beautiful creatures that unknowingly fell into Sharkley's trap as they were pursued.

"Sit down kids," George said, rubbing his chin with his hand. "I have something important to tell you about Sharkley that few people know." He sat at the foot of a flat rock and the three kids sat around him in a semicircle. They were watching him curiously.

"Sharkley's great grandfather, Captain Tom Sharkley, was known by many people of the world for his skills at hunting down whales. Back in the late 1800s, his reputation for bringing in the most whales spread throughout the U.S. and across the globe. At that time, whaling was an important and needed trade. Whale oil and bones were in demand and used in the manufacture of products, including soap, perfume and countless other items."

"Captain Tom saw many battles with whales of all sizes. When his grandson, Theodore was born, he taught him from the time he was a tiny tot, everything about living a life at sea. The young Theodore Sharkley learned all about whaling from his grandfather. His own father was involved in the shipping industry but had no love for the sea. The child learned all he could from his grandfather. When his grandfather died, the boy was devastated.

After the whaling industry's decline, it gradually died out in the United States, but other countries continued to track down the whales. Theodore Sharkley made a permanent home in Norway, where whaling was still permitted and he continued to hunt whales for profit. By this time, whales, killed by diesel-powered boats that were actually factory ships, could be processed in one hour. That included removing all the valuable blubber and some of the bones that would be sold to other countries."

"Theodore, better known to us as 'Captain Sharkley' hunted and killed hundreds of whales. Young Sharkley's mother died in childbirth and his father and grandfather raised him. When the International Whaling Commission formed to regulate the killing of whales, Theodore, a young man then, continued to hunt them. He soon became obsessed with whales, and his thrill with hunting them changed him forever," George said, pausing a moment to look at the sky—a crisp and cloudless baby blue. Katey, Will and Bartholomew waited quietly for him to continue with the fascinating story.

"Sharkley learned about Whale Island through his

father, who had never actually ventured to the island. There were too many dangers involved. He was there on the ship when his own father sent a small crew to Whale Island. Not one member of that crew returned. Whale Island is more than just a legend. Some of the whalebones found here give the people who find them mysterious powers."

"It is said that certain fish and whales found near Whale Island know the way to a lost land with a civilization of people who live like no other people in the entire world. There are only two people who have been to Whale Island who came back alive to tell about it. One of them is an old woman who came to live on Green Cave Island. She told Sharkley how to get to Whale Island after he captured her and stole her map, which is the very map we have with us now. So you see why Sharkley wanted this map. He wants to get to those whalebones. The ones he is desperately seeking. But there is a catch. There is only one entrance to this island where you can get in without being torn apart by sharks, and there is one way off the island," George said. "And you better believe that Sharkley knows both ways. I think he is somewhere on this island," George finished, and then he leaned back, putting his hands behind his head.

They stared at him in awe. Will suddenly recalled the conversation that Sharkley had with Henshaw about the "old witch" of Green Cave Island. Sharkley took the map from that poor lady!

"Sharkley got the map from that lady he called the 'old witch' of Green Cave," he said. *"But why would she give up something as valuable as the map to someone like Sharkley?"* Will wondered.

"You're right Will," said Katey. "I remember Sharkley and Henshaw talking about that lady. But maybe she knew something else about the island that she didn't tell Sharkley," Katey said. "Maybe," said Will, deep in thought.

They rested for a little while longer, watching the sun's rays glistening on the water and thinking about what George had just told them. The blistering heat quickly dried their clothes as they turned their attention to the nearby hill, hoping they would soon find water. They gathered the rest of the long, grayish bones they found and put them together with the few supplies they had left. Opening the last two bottles of water, they shared it among themselves.

A silvery flash of movement in the water caught Katey's eye. She ran to the water's edge to see what it was. Two silver-green fish with blue eyes were darting side by side through the water. They were knower fish, they had to be! They looked exactly as Uncle Hughie had described them. Katey was so excited that she waved her arms in the air and yelled to Will.

"Will, quick, come over here!" she said, beckoning him to her with her hands.

Will ran to Katey's side and saw what caused her excitement. He pulled out his whistle and the fish swam closely by them, peering at them with the most beautiful blue-green eyes Katey had ever seen on a fish. As the fish slowed and gently swam near them, one of them gurgled strange sounds. *What is this? Are they trying to tell us something?* Will tensed his body and strained to hear them as he stepped closer. The fish did not swim away. Instead, they opened their mouths and more garbled sounds spilled out. The sounds were jumbled at first, and the gurgle of the water made it more difficult to understand what the fish were saying.

"They're trying to say something!" Will said, concentrating on the strange sounds. As he strained to listen, he saw the bigger one open and close its mouth several times. Gurgling sounds made bubbles in the water. But then they heard it! It sounded like someone trying to talk under water. They were sure they heard real words!

The bigger fish examined Will with its intense, intelligent eyes and a string of words spilled into the water. He began to understand what it was saying.

"You have two things with you that will help you," the fish said to them. "The strange noise that comes from your whistle can be heard by all living things, with the exception of humans. You were able to get this far on the island because these sounds can kill sharks and a few other species of underwater inhabitants. The whistle's sound is painful to the sharks' auditory system. That is why they swam away from you." As they watched the fish closely, it paused for a second and continued.

"You must find Naleen, the whale who lives on this island. She will help you find an underground city located under the depths of the ocean floor. But she can only help you if you have the bones with you, the ones you found on these very shores. This underground city is the key to getting back to your home, and to finding your uncle, who is not lost at sea, as you might have imagined. You will go to Lolipolis, the city under the sea. And, to be sure, you will never forget it the rest of your lives. You will pass on what you learn to your children and grandchildren. But remember this! Be careful of the one with the long black hair and one clear eye!" Then they swam off, silver and green flashes of scaly bodies moving swiftly and gracefully back into the deeper waters of the lagoon.

Will and Katey were speechless. Uncle Hughie was not

dead, as they had thought! After the boat capsized, Will was sure he was lost at sea. Katey squealed with delight upon hearing that Uncle Hughie was alive. With a sudden burst of energy, she sprang up and ran up and down the shores of the lagoon. She was filled with a happiness that she hadn't felt in a long time. She whooped, gales of laughter bubbling from her mouth.

Will, still caught up in his own shock upon hearing the news, began to shake his head in disbelief. "Could he really be alive?" he thought aloud, the words tumbling excitedly from his mouth. As the fish's words slowly sunk in, he began to smile and he ran to Katey, spun her around, and the two danced in their delight. While he and Katey spun around crazily, George and Bartholomew watched in bewilderment, several yards away. "He's alive! He's alive!" they sang, jumping up and down with joy.

Then Katey explained to George and Bartholomew everything they learned from the knower fish. They began by telling them when they first saw the strange-looking fish with Uncle Hughie.

"The knower fish told us that Uncle Hughie survived the storm in Cape Cod! The first time we saw the fish was at Green Cave Island with Uncle Hughie, just before the storm capsized his boat," said Katey, her face brightly lit from learning that Uncle Hughie was alive somewhere on Whale Island. "The bigger knower fish with the blue-green eyes told us that we had to find a whale named 'Naleen.'"

Visions of the boat catapulting out to sea still gave Katey nightmares. But that time seemed so long ago. Now that they knew their uncle was alive, their spirits lifted and they knew they would find him soon.

Bartholomew wondered if they were making up this incredulous story about the knower fish. "Either I'm losing my hearing or you're losing your minds," he said, shaking his head and staring at them with a look that registered disbelief.

"But it's true! Uncle Hughie said that knower fish are rare and are important to finding a lost city under the depths of the sea, and he was right," Katey explained, seeing that Bartholomew still didn't seem to believe them. "Those fish just told us that there is a lost city, and we *must* find it. When we do, we'll find Uncle Hughie too. I just knew it! I knew all along that Uncle Hughie was still alive," she said.

"The knower fish told us to be wary of the one with the long black hair and one clear eye," added Will. "There's only one person I know that fits that description," Will said, his expression now serious. "Sharkley!" they all said in unison, glancing from one to the other.

CHAPTER 11

JAWS OF A KOMODO DRAGON

Venturing toward the hill, the foursome went in search of food and water. It was vital that they find food soon to give them renewed energy and satisfy their increasing hunger. The lagoon was far behind them now and they looked at the green landscape before them.

Suddenly, the ground started to shake slightly and the air was filled with a low rumbling sound. George knew instantly what it was.

"Get down low to the ground," he said, spreading his body flat on the grass. After about two minutes of rumbling and a slight movement of the ground below them, it finally stopped.

"Was that an earthquake?" Will asked, as he and Katey slowly and cautiously rose to their feet.

"We're in Indonesia, a place with many islands, well known for its volcanoes. There are still many active ones," George replied. "Volcanic eruptions aren't uncommon. In fact, earthquakes are a likely part of daily life here."

Katey was amazed by the different sizes of the mountains and neighboring volcanoes. Slowly, they all began walking toward the hill, searching everywhere for food. Huge trees, some one hundred eighty feet high, spread throughout the lush rain forest. Mango fruit hung from trees on which they flourished abundantly. The trees grew densely throughout the forest.

They reached for the mangos and hungrily plucked the ripe fruit, curiously realizing that many clusters sprang from its branches. They ate until they could not ingest another morsel. Satisfied, and hydrated by the delicious fruit, they moved on. Although the juice from the mangos helped to quench their thirst, George knew they would dehydrate from the heat if they did not find water soon.

The sky darkened and Katey heard rumbling noises again. The thought of another earthquake made her heart skip a beat. George noticed the alarm in her face and put a comforting hand on her shoulder.

"No need to worry. It's just thunder, Katey." He looked pensively at the gray sky. "It looks like we'll be getting some rain," George said, as the thick dark clouds seemed to loom even closer. He quickly cut the tops off of the four empty water bottles and returned them to the pillowcases. "We only need one pillowcase now. Our supplies have dwindled down considerably," he said, shaking the pillowcase to see what was left of their food supplies. He removed the sparse items from one pillowcase and emptied them into the other one. "It might come in handy, but it would be easier to carry one bag of supplies," he said, as he folded the unused one and carefully placed it inside the other pillowcase.

The skies opened and the rain poured steadily, drenching them, so they ran to the only place where they could find shelter. On the other side of the lagoon was another opening that led to a cave. They ran toward the cave to escape the pounding rain. A warm wind was blowing and tree branches blew crazily back and forth against the sky, which was now covered with the thick patches of gray clouds. When they reached the cave, George stepped in first, carrying the flashlight. But the flashlight no longer worked, waterlogged from the other cave.

They got lucky. The cave was only about twenty feet

deep and because it was still daylight, George could see it did not stretch back too far. The back of the cave was sealed off by a large pile of rocks. It was just big enough for them to escape the rain, and it looked safe. George ushered them in after checking it thoroughly.

They were glad to get out of the rain for a while, although it did help to cool them from the sweltering heat. Opening the pillowcase, he rummaged around until he found the four empty bottles with the cutoff tops. He stood the bottles up just outside the cave entrance and held them until they filled with rainwater. The water gathered quickly in the downpour. Katey, her hair soaked by the heavy rain, thought George was very smart to think of it, especially since they had nearly run out of water.

This cave was small and free of the rock formations they found in the other cave, but colorful marine algae adorned its ceiling and walls. It was a comfortable place to stay while they waited out the rain. They watched as raindrops splashed the surface of the turquoise-blue lagoon waters, the steady sound soothing them as it continued to pour down. Thunderous roars clapped overhead and lightning lit up the dark sky with streaks of bright light. Katey had flashbacks of the terrible storm that capsized Uncle Hughie's boat, and remembered another dark day on the ship.

"I'm glad we're not on Sharkley's ship," Katey said, shivering, arms crossed over her chest. She remembered how angry the skies looked on the day they were on Uncle Hughie's boat out on Cape Cod Bay. Katey glanced at Will who was mesmerized by the large pellets of falling rain. He was absorbed in his own thoughts. Katey drifted off to sleep and dreamt about a beautiful island with dolphins and whales who spoke to them as they swam in the blue-green water.

When the rain stopped, they gathered up their belongings and thirstily drank the water that had filled the empty bottles. Then they ate more of the mangos they collected earlier and gathered up their belongings. It was time to head back to the rain forest.

The forest was heavy with moisture, droplets of rain forming on every leaf they passed.

They were glad that the humidity dropped and they were feeling refreshed. They knew the stifling heat would return, so they walked quickly through the forest. Hearing the chirping of small animals, they looked up just in time to see a flight of colorful birds. As they walked a little further on, Katey was delighted to see tiny deer dart quickly past them, the same small deer they saw on the other side of the island. She tried to catch up to them, but they were too quick for her.

"Katey," Will shouted, concerned as he watched her move farther ahead of them. "Remember, we have to stick together here, because we don't know what dangers lay ahead!"

She slowed her steps and waited for the rest to catch up. Bartholomew, examining the trees, saw from the corner of his eye a greenish-brown movement high above them and turned his head up to see two lizards perched on the fat limbs.

"Those are young Komodo dragons," said George, as he reached Bartholomew's side. "They hide in the trees because they are easy prey to the large ones. But where there are small ones, there could also be adult dragons lurking around. Let's find a dry branch and light a torch to protect ourselves."

George knew they would be in grave danger if an adult dragon came by now. At least a fire would offer some protection. He touched his belt where he had tucked away his knife. He felt the sheath of the knife and kept his hand tightly wrapped around it, as if expecting to see a Komodo dragon appear.

They went in search of dry branches but found none, guardedly staying alert for dragons. They spotted an enormous tree that had fallen during a storm and searched under its long base for dry branches. They were in luck!

Several branches had broken off and although they were damp, they were not rain-soaked. George picked up two branches, discarding one. Then they heard a terrible sound, even as George was still examining the tree branch. Startled, he dropped it. The noise made Katey's heart leap in fear. Bartholomew stopped in his tracks too, frozen by the sound he just heard.

Behind them, a monstrous-looking Komodo dragon was storming in their direction. Brownish gray, its long, yellow tongue darting in and out of its mouth, it had to be fifteen feet in length, more than twice the size of George. And it made its deadly presence known.

George, seeing the huge animal gaining on them, dropped the branch he was holding. The others were shocked by the huge creature that was behind them.

"Everyone, run to the nearest tree that you can find and climb as high as you can," he said, beginning to run. Katey found the tree first. Its low, thick branches helped her climb to the top quickly. She climbed as high as she could, the others not far behind. George was the last, but his foot slipped and he fell to the ground. The dragon's huge mouth was open, revealing a forked yellow tongue and razor-sharp teeth. It was so close to George that he could almost reach out and touch it if he wanted.

The large creature was closing in on George quickly, but George rolled his body away from its powerful jaws in just enough time to escape the beast. The ghastly-looking creature's huge mouth was open, displaying daggerlike teeth which sought to clamp down on George's nearest body part.

Reflexively, George grabbed his knife from its sheath inside his belt buckle. Pulling it out in one quick motion, he jabbed at the dragon but the knife missed its mark. Terrified by the size of the dragon and its razor-sharp teeth, he focused every ounce of his brain on the fearful predator. He raised his arm again, ready to plunge the knife in the beast's side and then . . . the creature stopped *abruptly*! It stood rock-still. With the beast seemingly confused, George took his opportunity to attack. In one sweeping motion, George plunged the knife into its back. Blood gushed from the wound and it screamed in pain. The piercing cry echoed through the air and frightened the birds who took flight from the trees where they rested. They fluttered away, scattering in different directions.

In a final burst of energy, the dragon lurched again at George who scrambled backward to escape its wrath. The wounded animal continued to move angrily toward George. As it closed in, George stealthily took aim with his knife. The knife made its mark in the dragon's eye. Pitching forward with a jerk, it exhaled a last ragged breath, and then it was still.

Katey had covered her ears. The awful sounds emitted by the dying dragon reminded her of all the dinosaur movies she had ever seen. But those were not real—this was really happening! This dinosaur-like creature roared like those big beasts from which it was a descendent. She shuddered to think about what could have happened if George had not had his knife with him.

Exhausted, George fell to the ground near the lifeless dragon. Its fearsome mouth was still open. Blood was oozing from the dead creature's eye, trickling down its head and neck. Katey, Will and Bartholomew climbed down from the tree, relieved to see that their friend was unhurt. Katey ran to George's side, hugging him. "Are you okay, George? I was so afraid you would be killed."

George stood up. He was a bit wobbly but he looked down at the dead Komodo dragon. It could have killed him, if not for one lucky moment.

"Did you see when the dragon froze? It was just for a second or two but then it stopped and gave me time to get away. No telling what damage those mighty jaws and teeth would have done," George said, shaking his head, a look of sheer amazement on his face. "I thought I was going to be its next meal."

Will knew why the dragon stopped moving. He pulled the whistle out from his pocket where he had just replaced it and held it up.

"I took the whistle out and tried it on the dragon! I knew that if I didn't at least try, we might not be here talking to you now," Will said, returning the whistle to his pocket.

"I watched the dragon stop in its tracks. If it wasn't for that . . ." George's voice trailed off as he thought about what would have happened if the dragon made its mark. Surely, these kids would not survive this island on their own, he thought. "Thanks, Will," George said, extending his hand to shake Will's.

Turning around to look at the rain forest and the lush greenery, George realized they would have to take leave of it soon. "We have to get out of this forest and make our way to the other side of that mountain," George said, still breathing hard from his ordeal.

"Are you sure you're all right, George? Maybe we should take a break before moving on." Katey said, scrutinizing his face, which was flushed and covered with perspiration. "I'm okay, now, Katey," George replied, wiping the sweat from his face.

"Sure, now that he knows he has all his body parts intact," said Bartholomew, still gazing at the dead creature at their feet. Staring at the monster on the ground, Will thought it didn't look as fearsome dead as it did when it was alive.

"I think this will be our first real meal," George said, examining the carcass that lay limp on the ground. "We have to eat something other than berries and mangos, and until we find other food, this will have to do."

Katey's face blanched at the thought of eating it. She was not so sure she could eat a giant lizard, but hunger made them realize what they had to do. George retrieved his knife from the dragon's back and together, Will, George and Bartholomew turned it over so its belly was facing up. The underside was softer, and George knew it would be the more tender part of the animal. He began cutting and tearing large pieces of the dragon with his knife. Katey turned her face away, not wishing to see the blood and skin being torn from the dead animal. In the meantime, Will and Bartholomew found some large pieces of wood to start a fire.

After the fire was going strong, they feasted on the dragon in an enclosed area of the rain forest, filling their empty stomachs until they thought they would burst. The fire made them feel protected as the wonderful aroma of cooked food filled the air. Curiously, the dragon tasted wonderful.

"Isn't it strange to think that we're eating a creature that was related to dinosaurs," remarked Katey.

"It sure doesn't taste like a dinosaur," said Bartholomew, who was still shoveling food into his mouth.

"Well, how in the world do you know how a dinosaur tastes?" asked Katey, who grinned upon hearing the silly remark. They all roared with laughter at this. Bartholomew made a face at Katey, which she returned with a grin.

They felt content, and now that their hunger was abated, they talked about their next course of action. They remained watchful of their surroundings. This last experience with the Komodo dragon taught them that they would always have to be on their guard.

After they ate, they drank some of the rainwater that pooled on giant leaves, which were as big as a small child. Then they began their journey to the mountain. According to the map, this mountain was their destination. But what they would find there, none of them knew for sure. One thing was certain—they had to find water.

It was hot on this tropical island and they soon grew

tired, irritated and thirsty.

They were aware that they had to find the whale, Naleen, the one the knower fish told them about. Will wondered about Naleen, the whale that was supposed to help them. *But how would they know where to find Naleen?* He thought again about the watery message from the knower fish. Will knew that the whistle and the whalebones they found were important and held the key to questions that remained unanswered. They began the trek to the mountain and hoped they would find some answers there.

CHAPTER 12

THE MOUNTAIN

Walking together, they were amazed by the abundance of flora. The blooms that surrounded them in the lush rain forest were so beautiful that they made Katey gasp with pleasure. The large and exotic-looking Rafflesia they had seen on another part of the island was also growing on the landscape here. They could smell its distinct odor, which remarkably reminded them of rotting meat.

"It's too bad a flower so unusual and pretty smells so awful," Katey said, making a wide circle around one to avoid touching it. When they came upon some more Rafflesia, they avoided those too. The odor emanating from them was not appealing, except possibly to flies.

Orchids were also abundant and they came in all shapes and sizes, from the tiny, edible type to the large Tiger Orchid. George showed them how to eat the tiny orchid flower. Although it was not among their favorite food, they learned how to eat it and picked others to include with their dwindling food supplies.

To their delight, they came upon a grove of banana trees. As they excitedly picked the ripe ones from the bunches of fruit dangling in front of their faces, shy orangutans with blazing orange fur watched them curiously from the trees. One jumped from branch to branch as they passed by. They collected as many ripe bananas as they could for later, only too glad to be eating other types of fruit in addition to the mangos they found throughout the island.

Continuing to walk for another two hours, they came upon a stream that flowed into a large bed of water. They sprinted over to the inviting water. Quickly untying their shoes, they jumped in, fully clothed. The water felt refreshing as they scrubbed to get the grungy feeling of sweat intermingled with dirt off their bodies and clothes. The tepid waters were the perfect antidote to their tired, sweaty bodies. They drank from it, not caring whether or not it was good.

"This is the best water I've had in a long time!" said Katey, cupping her hands to get another drink. Will and Bartholomew were gulping down the water as if it was the last they would ever have. It tasted wonderful and they drank until they could drink no more. After having their fill, they playfully splashed each other and played a game of water tag.

Katey and Will walked back to a grassy area sprinkled with white sand. They lay back on large rocks by the riverbed, relaxing and letting the hot sun dry their wet clothes.

"Will," said Katey, dreamily staring at the cloudless blue sky, "Do you miss Dad?"

"Yeah, Katey, I do," he said. "I think about him a lot. You know, it's been six weeks since we've been gone, and soon school will begin. It's hard to believe that we've been away from home that long," he said.

"I know. I miss Gobie, too," Katey said, her eyes filling with a yearning. He put his arm around her.

"Katey, we have each other. I know we're going to make it home and see Dad again . . . and soon," he added. They sat like this for a while, glad to have each other and both dreaming they would find their way back home. Finally, Will stood, removing the whistle from his pocket. Something else fell out of his pocket. He bent to pick up the long, gray whalebone they found at the lagoon. He examined it and felt it had some mysterious power.

"Boy, will *we* ever have some adventure story to tell Uncle Hughie when we see him. He thinks he's had some adventures. Well, this one tops them all!" said Will, laughing and returning the whalebone to his pocket. Katey giggled at the thought of the expression on Uncle Hughie's face when they tell him about the Komodo dragons and the escape from Sharkley's ship. She sighed, letting the sun bask her face with its warmth, and in minutes, she fell asleep, dreaming of her father and Uncle Hughie sitting on the front porch at home.

She woke up to see the descending sun, filling the sky with a streaky orange glow. Her clothes had dried in the heat of the day, her face pink from the sun. It must be late, she thought. Turning her eyes to the water where they bathed earlier, she saw Will and George at the foot of the river. They stood knee deep in water, their pant legs torn off above the knees. Bartholomew was sound asleep on another rock near the huge rock where she had fallen asleep. His legs askew, one arm was thrown over his head and the other at his side. He looks so peaceful, thought Katey. This is probably the happiest we've been since we arrived on this island. So much has happened. She stretched her arms up toward the sky, sat up, and looked at the glistening water in the late afternoon sun.

She meandered over to Will and George. They were fashioning spears out of long tree branches. George was whittling the top of a long, thin branch he had found. The wood looked raw and sharp where he had shaped it into a point. He was almost finished, working hard to sharpen it. Will had buried two lighted torches in the sand. She knew they couldn't be without a torch or a spear, especially if a dangerous animal happened upon them again.

"What have you two been up to?" asked Katey, watching George skillfully carve one end of the branch into a sharp point.

"We want to catch some fish to eat later," said George. "We're all getting tired of fruit and the dragon meat was spoiled. It was exposed to the heat, attracting bugs and scavengers, so we got rid of it."

"We'll have to find some shelter before dark," George continued. "We can't risk exposing ourselves to stray wildlife."

Will busily gathered sticks and small branches for the fire they would build later. He looked up, saw Katey, and walked over to her.

"How are you feeling, Katey?" Will asked. "You and

Bartholomew looked so tired that I didn't want to wake you up. While you were sleeping, George finished working on the spears, and I found a spot that could provide us with shelter for the night."

"Let's take a look at it, Will," said George, Katey nodding her head in agreement. "How far is it?"

"Just a little way off down the riverbed," Will replied. "But we can't leave Katey alone. Let's wake up Sleeping Beauty over there," Will said.

Will shook Bartholomew awake. *"Hu–h–h–h . . .* what's happening?" Bartholomew said. He rubbed his eyes and stretched out his arms. "I was just dreaming about eating a big roasted chicken that was dripping with butter and potatoes on the side," he said. "It was a great dream. Why did you have to wake me up? I was just about it eat it."

"It's time to get up! You and Katey have to stand watch. George and I are going to explore a spot I found that could be a possible shelter for us tonight," Will said, handing him one of the torches. "Use this if you need to. Look, George made a spear. He's making another one out of the other branch. You hold onto this one, just in case, until George and I return."

"Aye, aye, captain," Bartholomew said, in a mock salute. He grinned and took the spear from Will's hand. He gave the torch to Katey, who put it back into the hole in the sand as they walked to the river. Wading in only up to their knees, Katey and Bartholomew searched the water for fish. "Be back soon," Will yelled, as he made his way to the shelter he found earlier.

George and Will walked a distance equal to about half a mile when Will saw the overhang he had come upon earlier. It was a long flat rock that jutted out above a grassy clearing and it was surrounded by trees. Next to the clearing was a small stream that flowed back into the river. The long flat rock was big enough to protect them from rain and they could create makeshift beds with some of the large leaves from the forest.

"This will do just fine," George said, approving of Will's choice. They dumped the sticks and large branches they gathered earlier and stored them under the rock. They would need their equipment to make a fire when they came back with Katey and Bartholomew. Nightfall would arrive in about two hours, so they worked quickly. They headed back when they were finished.

When Bartholomew saw Will and George approach, he waved the spear at them. On the spear was a huge fish. Bartholomew, beaming with pride, held the wooden stick up high. He learned how to throw a spear from Big Anthony when he was on his uncle's ship. Big Anthony taught him how to fish on Sharkley's whaling voyages. He was almost an expert at spearing fish. Big Anthony was probably the only person on the ship Bartholomew befriended. Now he could safely include George in that category.

As he waved the fish in their faces, Will grinned, slapping him on the back in camaraderie.

"Hey, that's awesome!" said Will. He playfully tried to grab the spear from Bartholomew, but he stepped aside and Will tripped on a rock, falling into the water. He came up sputtering and laughing, then pushed Bartholomew down, which loosened the spear from his grip. George grabbed it before it was carried off in the fast-moving stream and they all began to rumble with laughter.

"Hey, if you lost our meal, I would have made you pay!" Bartholomew said, pushing his wet hair back off his forehead.

"All I have that's worth anything are these old sneakers. You can have them!" said Will, snorting with laughter again. "They're a lot better than those weird shoes you're wearing!" Then they dried themselves off and gathered up the supplies and torches and walked to the rock shelter Will found.

When they arrived, Katey thought it was perfect. "It

even has a little stream of water nearby where we can drink and wash," she said. "And tonight we'll eat fish and bananas for dinner. What a funny combination!"

They began gathering the giant-sized leaves from the nearby trees and prepared their beds. Katey examined the leaves, checking for any bugs that could be hiding under them. She imagined finding bugs crawling on her in the night, although she knew the fire that George made would keep most bugs and animals away.

Katey wanted to explore the area around the shelter, so she took a torch and she and Bartholomew walked up the incline above the rock. In the distance, she saw a big mountain with tall peaks. It was the mountain they would explore tomorrow, the one on the map.

Volcanoes, wisps of smoke curling from their openings, lay just behind the mountain. Lush greenery was everywhere. The ocean's crisp blue-green waters were shimmering in the distance and it seemed to surround the mountain. It was a breathtaking view. Darkness would be descending soon. They knew they would have to get back to the shelter before nightfall.

"Stay together and don't go wandering far," Will shouted, warning both of them. Bartholomew promised to be back in a short time. Will knew that being out after nightfall was not wise, especially when this turf belonged to such a wide variety of unusual animals. Although Whale Island was beautiful, it was dangerous, and inhabited by so many different animals and plant life. These creatures knew their territory much better than they did. Will watched them walk farther, until they were two small shapes disappearing from view. Then he turned around to help George get the fire ready.

Katey climbed up the hill, Bartholomew just behind her. At the top was a grassy plain scattered with trees and flowers. A few of the small deer they had seen in the rain forest were meandering around the clearing, their eyes and ears sensitive to danger. They watched the tiny creatures, no bigger than a medium-sized dog, and marveled at their miniature bodies. The deer seemed to sense them and ran away into the thick forest.

A lizard scuttled in front of them, no bigger than Katey's index finger. It looked like Rex, the little lizard she found on the other side of the island. She ran after it, but it darted out of her reach, just as she lay a finger on its tiny tail. She was determined to get him.

"Come back here little one," she said, running to catch up, but it scurried away behind a tree. Concentrating on finding the lizard, she did not immediately notice the shoe sticking out from behind the tree. When she approached the tree, she was surprised to see a lifeless body sprawled on the ground. She clasped her hand over her mouth, not realizing that a scream had escaped. Frozen in place, she stared at the dreadful sight. Bartholomew, hearing her scream, ran to her side, the torch still blazing in his hand.

Katey was shaking as she pointed to the unmoving figure. It was the body of a man with dark hair. A second shoe peeked out from under the ragged, shredded pants. A green and black shirt, faded and ripped, partially covered the torso. One arm had been torn from its socket. It was a frightful sight with flies buzzing around its face. The stench of death was overwhelming.

"Whoa!" Bartholomew said, dropping to his knees near the corpse and holding his nose to ward off the foul smell of decomposition. He quickly got up on shaky legs and vomited his entire last meal. After recovering, he wiped his mouth with the back of his hand and scrutinized the dead man's face.

"This is Scally, I'm positive of it! Look at his shirt. It's ripped, looks almost like a large bite mark. An animal nearly took off his arm."

Katey was shocked to see that it really was Scally, now a lifeless form that looked so different from the way she remembered him on the ship. She turned her head away from the gruesome scene, covering her nose and mouth to ward off the unpleasant odor.

"We better get back to Will and George and show them what we've found," Katey said. "You're right, Katey, let's go before it gets dark," Bartholomew answered, as he turned in the direction of the shelter. Two figures were running toward them.

Will was nearly at their sides, with George straggling behind. Both of them heard Katey's scream back at the shelter. George had his knife in one hand, a lighted torch in the other. When they saw Katey and Bartholomew's expressions, they knew something was terribly wrong.

"What happened, Katey?" Will asked her, noticing that her face had turned white. "We heard you scream," he said, visibly shaken. His face was flushed and he had his whistle out in his hand.

"Will, look," she said, pointing to the corpse. But George had already seen it and emitted a low whistle, accompanied by a look of astonishment. He slowly walked toward the body and examined it carefully.

"It's Scally. He was probably on his way to the mountain," George said. "He hasn't been dead that long. Maybe a day or two. Looks like a deep wound to his head," he added, pointing to the hole in the back of his skull, caked with dried blood. "Either he was hit with something sharp or he fell and hit his head. If he was hit, the poor guy probably didn't even know it was coming. The animals got to him later."

They watched solemnly as he placed the lifeless head back on the ground. "We should bury him. Scally deserves at least that after what he's been through," George said. "You know what this means, don't you? It means Sharkley and his men are somewhere on this island," he added, looking intently at each of their faces to make sure his words would sink in. "We'll need eyes and ears behind our heads now too."

They found a good spot next to a young tree and the four of them dug a hole with the spears, their hands, and any large tree branches they could find. Removing his shoes, George then placed the body into the grave. They said a prayer before leaving, and walked in silence back to the shelter.

The dusky evening sky was now beginning to turn bluish gray. Night would be upon them soon and they had to get back to their safe place for the night. Tomorrow they would journey to the mountain. Maybe they would find some answers there. Katey wasn't entirely sure if she wanted to know the answers now. An uneasy feeling crept into her head and she anxiously wondered what else they might stumble upon.

The fire George made was comforting. Silent now, they purposely avoided talking about their horrible discovery, but it lingered in their minds. They ate the fish that Bartholomew had caught earlier. George cooked it over the fire until it was crispy on the outside and tender inside. Feasting on the tasty meal, they pulled out some of the bananas they had collected from the forest, and drank from the nearby stream.

Will, finishing the last bite of fish, was the first to break the silence. Gazing thoughtfully into the fire, he said, "We have to have a plan, especially after what happened to Scally. And I think finding Naleen is a big part of the plan. The knower fish told us that Naleen is the whale who will help us get to the lost city and Uncle Hughie."

"I'm convinced now that the whalebones we found have never been seen by anyone else. And that we were able to get to Whale Island because we have this whistle. I know it. I think others who tried to get on the island couldn't have made it," Will finished. He held the whistle up in his hand now and stared at it thoughtfully, the fire casting shadows on a face deep in thought.

"You are right, Will," said George. "A big ship couldn't get past those big craggy rocks. And even if they tried to go to the island with lifeboats, they wouldn't have made it past the sharks. Those deadly sharks. You saw what they did to the boat. We almost didn't make it here either."

"That's probably why this island is inhabited only by animals. But somehow, Sharkley and some of his crew made it; I don't know how, but they made it here," George finished.

Bartholomew agreed. He knew that Will was right. He knew about all the ships and the people on those ships who tried to get to the island and never returned. Sharkley knew too.

"*No one* who attempted to get to Whale Island has ever returned alive. Not many people even know of its existence. Without Sharkley's map, there's no way anyone would find their way on this island, especially since there's only one real way in," Bartholomew said, gesturing to the mountain towering over them.

Sharkley knew, George thought. He memorized the map and then he let them steal it. George knew in his heart they'd meet up with him again—they hadn't seen the last of that tyrant.

CHAPTER 13

NALEEN

Weary and uneasy after their gruesome find, they talked for hours about what they would do when they finally reached their destination, and agreed that they should finalize their plans before they started out in the morning.

Despite the many different types of animals about, there was something ominous in the air and it had nothing to do with the creatures that roamed the island. By the looks of poor Scally, they were in danger too. The little comfort they took came from the words of the knower fish, and they were quite sure the whalebones they found at the lagoon were important.

"We have to find Naleen," said Katey, her eyes fastened on the firelight. "Naleen will help us find our way home." They all looked at her, and hoped she was right.

The youngsters fell into a light and dreamless sleep. He watched the three peaceful faces relaxed in sleep, but George remained awake, his mind churning. He stirred the fire and kept it brightly lit throughout the night. He was aware of every movement and sound. He heard every snap and rustle of the animals that seemed to surround them in the night.

George recalled Scally's body and how they had discovered it. Worry lines creased his brow. Scally was surely on his way to the mountain, George thought. But what was he doing there and was he alone? Someone or something was determined to not let anyone leave the island. Thoughts were running crazily through his head and he knew he would have a hard time falling asleep.

He watched the moonlight in the dark night sky, his weary eyes beginning to close. Finally, he fell into an uneasy sleep and dreamed about a dark, looming figure, but couldn't see the face of the villain.

They woke in the morning, eager and ready to begin walking to the mountain. Will and George had taken out the map and were busy examining it. Will pointed to a dark spot on the map and wondered what it meant.

"Look at this spot that Sharkley marked on the map. It must mean that this is the entranceway to the mountain. What do you think, George?" Will asked him.

George studied the map and handed it back to Will. "This looks like the entrance," he said, noting the volcanoes in the distance, which were spitting tufts of smoke into the air. "We must be careful. The volcanoes in this area are still active."

After a light breakfast of bananas and mangos, they set out for their destination. Careful not to stray away from each other, they stopped to look at the gravesite where they buried Scally's body yesterday before they continued to walk in heavy silence toward the mountain. Slight rumbling noises were coming from the volcano that was closest to the mountain. It reminded Katey of the first day on the island when they were caught in an earthquake.

The sky was overcast, grayish, and a few dark clouds scattered here and there. Katey, renewed from a good night's sleep, chattered happily and wondered what secrets they were about to uncover. The water surrounding the mountain looked darker today than it did yesterday and matched George's mood. After a night without sleep, his scowl was deeper than ever. Katey tried to lighten his dark mood with chatter but he remained quieter than usual. She noticed that he kept his knife on his belt buckle in a spot that was easily accessible. His scowl lines deepened when he was upset or worried. Today he looked angry, distant and guarded.

The birds that made their home in the rain forest were noisier than usual. Beautiful birds of paradise moved in a strange dance-like walk, showing off long plumes of bright colors. Peacocks were also abundant, the males strutting tall and proud, fanning their colorful feathers at the less attractive females.

Blooms of colorful flowers grew as far as the eye could see. Green plants, shrubs and trees made a lush blanket of natural beauty that spread across the forest landscape. Some of the trees were bigger than any they had seen before. The odd aroma of the huge Rafflesia flower, with its dazzling red bloom with white specks was also common in this part of the forest, although they stayed away from it. They knew that flower well. Its distinctive smell reminded Katey of decayed meat. She held her nose as she passed it.

Bartholomew held the spear in ready position by his side, confident in knowing his aim was usually on the mark. They stopped only once to drink from a stream that flowed from a twenty foot high rock waterfall. Behind the waterfall, a spectacular rainbow displayed muted colors that ended at a bubbling stream. Although the stream was warm, they were thirsty and they greedily drank from it. It was midmorning but the heat was almost unbearable, slowing them down and making them thirsty.

Above them, the rumbling from the volcano was louder. Katey warily watched the rings of smoke rise from a cone-shaped volcano. She longed to be anywhere but where they were right now. Bartholomew was walking side by side with her; Will and George were two steps ahead of them.

"We should hurry, don't you think, Bartholomew?" Katey said, anxiously watching the swirling smoke that rose up around the top of the volcano. Bartholomew studied her face. "Are you scared, Katey?" he asked, a mischievous curl pulling at the corner of his mouth.

"Look at that smoke . . . and don't you hear the noise? That volcano could erupt any time," Katey said, annoyed at him for making fun of her.

"I don't think so, Katey. Big eruptions are rare and remember what George said, this part of the world has active volcanoes. There are a lot of these islands with volcanoes all over the place."

"But what if we get caught in an eruption and another

earthquake? We could die here," Katey said, pushing her hair away from her face, which was shiny with sweat.

"Katey," Bartholomew said affectionately, "I won't let anything happen to you," and he playfully tugged her long hair. She retaliated by punching him and they soon both doubled up with laughter.

Will turned around and was glad to see that Katey was calmer than she had been the last two days. He knew she was homesick, but so was he. "What are you two up to?" said Will, grinning at them.

"Nothing," said Bartholomew. "Your sister is just beating me up, that's all." Giggling, she began to run ahead and Bartholomew followed, easily catching up to her and Will.

The sky was growing darker, the water surrounding the mountain matching the color of the sky. As they got closer to their destination, they stopped only to collect more fruit, which they found on the trees. Mangos, bananas and berries were abundant and they hungrily picked them and threw them in with their dwindling supplies. One of the big butterfly-moths they had seen several days ago was gingerly fluttering its six-inch wings of gold, blue and green, sitting peacefully in a flower. It almost looked like part of the flower petals on which it rested. It was startled at their approach, and Katey watched as it flew up into the sky.

Then she turned her attention to the freshly picked berries in her hand. They looked delicious and she nibbled at them as they continued in the direction of the mountain.

George was pensive and aware of every movement and rustling of the trees. Curious animals watched them as they walked past, and then, losing interest, disappeared into the forest again. A tiny lizard stood stone-still in the grass in front of them, and Katey caught it and held it in the palm of her hand. Not wanting to rest in one place for too long, it hopped out of her hand and scrambled along the ground back into the forest from which it came.

Rain fell from a sky dark with black clouds. The clouds covered the entire sky, making the midafternoon day seem like night. Streaks of lightening brightened patches of the dark sky, and Katey wished they were back in the shelter by the lagoon. The wind began to howl and branches swayed, like spindly arms reaching out toward the sky.

They soon reached the shore and found it riddled with rocks of all sizes. They stepped gingerly from each one, taking care not to fall on the jagged edges. An opening in the mountain was halfway filled with water, and through rain-soaked eyes, they thought they could see beyond it. The other side led to quiet surf and they did not know what lay in those waters beyond. Looking around for the best way to get through the opening, they realized they would have to swim. There was no other way to pass, as there were no forest paths here. Will nervously patted the whistle in his pocket, wondering if they would need it.

Katey secretly dreaded swimming, as she was not very good at it and hoped it would not take too long. Bartholomew would have to leave the spear behind, as he would not be able to swim with it.

"Will," said Katey, her voice barely a whisper, "Do you think there are any sharks in the water?" She was staring at the dark blue ripples, a twinge of fear in her eyes. Truth be told, Will was just as scared at the thought of coming face to face with a shark, but he put her mind at rest.

"Remember, Katey, the whistle helped us the first time we landed on the shores of this island. According to Sharkley's map, this is the best and only way to get onto the island," Will said, trying to comfort her with his words. "We have to get to the other side and it looks like this is the only way."

A rumbling noise, like thunder, echoed through the air. Suddenly, an explosion of orange-yellow sparks of molten lava spilled out of the mouth of the smoking volcano nearest the mountain. Bartholomew's mouth dropped in surprise and awe. He stood watching the sight. The first one to move was George.

"Let's go!" he yelled. "We'll have to swim to the other side. That lava is on its way down the volcano and could reach water soon. We have no choice but to go, *now!*" he said. "Katey, stay next to Will." Putting his hands on Katey's shoulders and turning her gently toward him, he looked her straight in the eyes. "Don't worry, remember, I'm right behind you," he said, picking up the supply case and hoisting it on his back.

"I'm not scared. As long as we're together," she said, with a brave tilt of her chin. Her words were braver than she actually felt.

Her mind drifted to thoughts of home: her soft and comfortable bed with the bedspread decorated with jungle animals; her dog, Gobie, whose affectionate kisses woke her every morning before school; the glistening waters of the bay, which she could see from her bedroom window. Her mother's smiling face in the photo on her nightstand and the warm, comforting face of her father, all appeared before her eyes. She let her imagination fill her mind and it helped her forget about where she was in the water.

The dark gray-blue water was warm, heated by the warmth of the earth's crust and the nearby volcano. The tepid waters were common to the Indonesian islands, which was close to the equator and sprinkled with the many volcanoes that sprawled across its landscape.

Swimming toward the sea cave, Will and George tried not to watch the tiny spurts of lava spilling out of the angry mouth of the volcano. Concentrating on getting to the cave on the other side, Will turned once to check on Katey. She was straggling behind, trying bravely to keep up with them. He knew she was terrified.

To their great surprise, a large black and white shape loomed up in front of them. Its long, shiny, thick body jumped gracefully out of the water. As it dove in head first, its twelve-foot fantail lifted majestically out of the water. This was a real whale! It was a humpback whale, the sleek black body and white pectoral fins making it seem like an angel of the water. Katey and Will had seen it before from the deck of the *Barking Barracuda.* Bartholomew had seen many humpback whales from his Uncle's whaling expeditions.

Although they were stunned by its sudden appearance, they were not afraid. The beautiful whale quietly surfaced under them, nudging them gently along. They found her fins and held fast to them as she glided across the water. In slow, rhythmic motions, they bypassed the cave as she brought them around to the other side of the mountain. Katey was surprised by the whale's intelligence and mild manner. What was most amazing is that she didn't feel afraid.

The water behind the mountain was not as warm, and the open sea was all they could see for miles. In the distant horizon, a scattering of many mountains and volcanoes of all sizes formed the vast Indonesian landscape.

The whale slowed her movements enough for them to hear the lovely whooshing sounds she made as she breathed, letting the characteristic spout of mist spray down on them from above. It felt surreal, as if they were in a dream, with a gentle giant steering them away from danger. Katey touched the round, bumpy knobs on its back and her heart soared with a sense of friendship to this creature of the ocean. Now she knew what Uncle Hughie meant when he spoke about how awesome it was to be near a whale. What was it he said? Katey remembered the look on his face when he said, "it felt like being in heaven," and that he was "a visitor" in the whale's home. She wondered what Uncle Hughie would do if he was as close as this. She chuckled at the thought.

The whale began to slow down and they heard a lovely sound that at once soothed and enchanted them. It was unlike any song they had ever heard. Although Bartholomew remembered hearing the magnificent music of these whales before, it was different than he recalled. This was the haunting, musical sound of several whales who were communicating with each other. The funny thing was that Katey thought she heard words coming from the whales. Will heard it too—they all did.

Suddenly, the whale's sounds became clear to them: they heard high, lilting tones and were awestruck upon hearing actual words from her.

"I am Naleen," said the magnificent creature. "You can understand what I am saying because of the long gray bones you carry, the ones you found at the lagoon. Only two others of your kind were able to leave this island with these bones. They are the bones of my forefathers. The bones give you the ability to hear and understand the language of my kind, the whales, dolphins, and other animals of this land. We have lived in these waters for many thousands of years. We have taught humans through the years how to speak and communicate with us."

"There are people of only one civilization who can communicate with us without the bones," Naleen explained. "They learned our language more than 9,000 years ago and their world is much different than the human world you know. I am going to take you there. It is a place of beauty and harmony such as you have never known. It is like the part of the universe in which the Creator lives. Two other humans who have been to my world are still there among my people. I live in a thriving city, hidden under the depths of the ocean. Some of the humans from your world are living there among my people. One of them is someone you know very well."

"Who is this person, the one you say we know?" Will asked, wondering who Naleen was talking about.

"You will learn soon enough," Naleen said, gently flipping the fin Will held. Fascinated by the experience of riding on a whale, he wondered why they were not slipping from the creature's giant wet body. He didn't have a chance to ask, as a school of striking-colored fish swam near and he watched them gently glide by. Katey was the first to introduce herself to Naleen.

"It is an honor to meet you," Katey began. "My name is Katey. This is my brother, Will, and our friends, Bartholomew and George. We have traveled many miles to get to this island. We learned about it from a very bad man named Captain Sharkley. He had the map of Whale Island and he knew about the bones you told us about. When we escaped from his ship, we took the map. George believes he's using us to get the bones. We think he intends to steal them from us."

"You are in grave danger," Naleen said, the words seeming to come from her blow hole and not the huge gaping mouth in which there were rows of long thin bones, much like the ones they found on the island.

"The man named Captain Sharkley has killed many whales and dolphins. He is known to us as 'the destroyer.' He would use the power of the bones to get to my world. He would take what he wants, ravage our lands and everything that is good and destroy it."

Will was listening intently to Naleen's words and wondered if the world she spoke of was the lost city, the one he read about in so many books. This city was destroyed thousands of years ago. "What is the name of the city you share with these people?" Will asked her.

"My world is called 'Lolipolis,'" she said, as her huge, sleek body swam toward the opposite end of the cave, "a city that nearly disappeared in an earthquake and tidal wave. The people who survived had the tools and technology to rebuild their city. They learned our language and how to speak to us. You can understand my language only because you are the holder of the bones. And this is only part of the power of the bones."

"There is one other thing you should know about them," Naleen said. "By holding one in your hand or putting it anywhere on your body, it will enable you to hold your breath under the ocean waters for many hours at a time. You will need to do this to get to my world. But you will have to learn the other powers by yourself. I am here to bring you to Lolipolis and help you to learn about the ways of my kind. One day in the future, your world will learn how to speak to us and we will all be in harmony."

Will remembered the whistle he had in his pocket. "What about this whistle I found at Green Cave Island? It lets us hear the words of fish and gathers animals close to us. The only sea life that won't come near us when I blow it are the sharks we encountered at the other end of Whale Island," he explained.

"The reason why the sharks do not come near at the sound of the whistle is because the frequency range causes them pain. That is why they turn away from you," Naleen explained. "The whistle belonged to a wise person who had the misfortune to meet Captain Sharkley. This wise woman was the sole possessor of the map of Whale Island, the one Sharkley took from her and that you now have with you."

"You're talking about the old witch of Green Cave Island!" Katey exclaimed, remembering Sharkley's words to Henshaw the night she discovered that he had the map. "Sharkley told Henshaw that he got the map from an old witch," Katey said, looking at Will.

"That's right," Will said. "I remember you telling us about it, and that's how you found out about the map."

"Sadly, the woman you are speaking of was someone who lived in our underworld city. There are only a few people on Lolipolis who willingly come to your world above the sea. This woman, Grĕta, was going to give the map to someone from your world who could be trusted with it. Sharkley found out about the map and found his way to the place you call Green Cave Island to retrieve it. Green Cave Island is the only other way to get to the lost city, but I cannot reveal how," Naleen said.

"Uncle Hughie was right!" Katey and Will exclaimed together, remembering his words when he told them that the knower fish at Green Cave would lead to a lost kingdom under the sea. "He knew that there was a city under the sea. We thought he was kidding us," Katey said with excitement, upon hearing Naleen's words.

Nodding her head in agreement, Naleen continued her tale. She told them how whales have highly sophisticated communication systems that enable them to speak to each other over vast distances and a frequency range well outside that of humans. She continued toward the cave, which they realized was very long. It would have taken them some time to get through it by themselves.

"We are going to the cave. There is a great hole under the depths of the sea, starting in this cave. That is the entranceway to my world," Naleen said.

Naleen asked each of them to hold a whalebone. Finding the bones in the supply case, George handed one to each of them. They each held it firmly in their pockets.

With a great splash, Naleen dove deep into bottom of the depths of the ocean, George, Will, Katey, and Bartholomew holding on to her fins and wondering how they were able to breathe underwater. They passed schools of fish, some strange-looking, with hard, rocklike bodies, flat ones with eyes on top of their heads, and others with bursts of color that flashed before their eyes. The long scary-looking ones with the sharp teeth did not enchant Katey. Naleen ignored all of the fish and continued swimming down to the ocean floor.

At the first dive into the ocean's depths, Katey felt a tightening in her chest and was afraid she would stop breathing and drown. But after she relaxed and enjoyed the ride, she hung onto Naleen's long fins, and felt better. She no longer needed to breathe and it was a strange feeling. It was as if all the oxygen in her chest was trapped in her lungs, until the time she would need it again.

Adjusting quickly to holding his breath, Will was amazed at the sights they saw on their way down to the ocean floor. His eyes nearly popped out of his head when they passed two sharks, which had no interest in them. They were blue sharks, fast swimmers that were not the largest and not the most aggressive of their species. Their empty, black eyes were searching everywhere for food and they moved in a rhythmic motion, never stopping. To Will, they seemed like cold, eating machines. He was fascinated by all that he took in around him, and he wondered what Katey was thinking. He would find out soon enough!

CHAPTER 14

LOLIPOLIS

The first thing that Bartholomew noticed was that he could open his eyes without feeling the weight of water in them. Usually, when he dove into deep water, he felt stinging and heaviness in his eyes if they were open, and he had to adjust to seeing everything around him. He felt as if he was in some kind of fantasy-like dream. Bartholomew had a hard time believing they were really swimming with a whale, and he felt like a fish. He did not even need an oxygen tank to breathe. "*How awesome is that!*" he thought. He looked up to see that they were now very far from the ocean's surface. Thinking about that scared him a little and he closed his eyes.

Curious fish of all sizes, shapes and colors swam near them, and then, as if bored by the strange-looking creatures that accompanied Naleen, turned and went about their business. They were only two feet away from the dark ocean floor when they came upon a wide, deep crevice at the bottom. The opening of the crevice, a gaping hole, was big enough to allow two whales to swim through it together. Like a wide tunnel, it was surrounded on both sides by the earth's crust and water. As they entered the opening, they immediately felt the rush of warm water all around them. The temperature of the water continued to rise as they neared the center of the earth.

They would never have found this opening on their own. Now Katey understood why the map was marked just at the spot where mountain and its cave joined. Only two people ever found their way to the lost city, Katey mused. She could see why it could be virtually impossible to get there without technological intervention or outside help from an even greater source. Katey knew that the bones and the magical powers which came from them were the reason why Naleen found them. Now, knowing they were the only ones, save for two others in the world who had the privilege of seeing "Lolipolis," it amazed and humbled them.

Swimming quickly through another tunnel-like opening that began to get brighter as they got closer to the end, they passed a second whale on its way to the ocean's surface. Naleen nudged the whale and flicked her tail in greeting. The other whale responded by opening his huge, gaping mouth, showing rows of long white-gray bones, and flicking its tail back.

The next sight was so incredible that if Katey could have gasped under water, she would have let out all of her breath. A brilliant dome-shaped building, immense in size, two miles long and several miles high was shimmering before their eyes. Shaped like a diamond, the wide, sprawling bottom of the structure appeared to almost float in place. It was reflecting thousands of particles of light and looked like a huge diamond with facets of shimmering light bouncing off its surface. Now Katey understood the reason why the tunnel seemed brighter as they reached the end.

Inside the diamond-shaped structure were buildings, of textures and materials that were not from the world as they knew it. There were circular roads and small rivers that fed into a larger body of water. As they got closer, they saw many dolphins and whales working alongside people. Naleen took them through another tunnel that opened into the diamond-shaped structure. They broke through the surface of a turquoise-blue waterway that was unique to the city of Lolipolis.

When they felt themselves bobbing above the surface of the crystal clear turquoise water, they were able to breathe normally again. Awed by the marvels before them, they could not believe their eyes. Whales and dolphins swam merrily past them, uttering greetings that they could understand. It was truly a remarkable place, as they were about to find out for themselves.

With a great, noisy spout of water, Naleen released a loud whoosh of spray through her blowhole. She took in deep breaths and released streams of mist in the air that rose up more than ten feet.

It took a few minutes for the four of them to adjust to breathing in the air. The pressure Katey felt in her chest was gone. She took in deep breaths and looked around at the vast beauty surrounding them.

The landscape before them was breathtaking. In the center of three alternating circles of land and sea stood a big mountain with trees, flowers and waterfalls. The waterfalls fed into a network of canals and the flourishing landscape was noticeably green. Surrounding them were lush emerald-green trees, bushes and grass. Tropical birds made their homes in the trees and sang songs of joy to each other, as well as to all that would listen.

In the center of the great mountain arose a huge building. It looked as big as a palace, large enough for hundreds of people to live together quite comfortably. It had towers, gates and parapets trimmed with gleaming brass, copper and tin, and was surrounded by a wall of gold. Huge statues made of gold were shining like the sun and scattered around the palatial building.

There were thermal baths and aqueducts, fountains and gardens on each ring of land, in addition to simple but elegantly-built homes and buildings where many of the citizens of the city lived.

In each canal of turquoise-blue water, there were many whales and dolphins. Boats also filled the canals and they were amazed to see people working busily together with whales to bring in cargoes from other lands. What truly stunned them was the affection and respect the people and whales displayed toward each other. It made the land seem like a paradise. Wild animals, such as giraffes, elephants and zebras, walked around the forests of the third ring of land and lived peacefully together, living on the plants and greenery that grew in abundance.

A long canal linked the city with the tunnel through which they came. This tunnel led to the open sea and several hidden canals linked each of the water rings to the city. Katey, Will and Bartholomew listened intently when they learned that there were two sea caves, one that was visible and the other that was hidden, formed over the years by the moving earth and volcanic eruptions. Both caves were located near the mountain and the volcano above the sea.

"The cave which is not visible at high tide can be seen only when the tide is low," explained Naleen. "Through that cave you will find the tunnel that leads to the diamond city, but it has not yet been discovered because very few people have been able to find it. Those who have made their way to Whale Island are usually killed by sharks or other wild animals before they even get that far," Naleen said.

"How did the diamond city get here?" Will asked.

"It was built many thousands of years ago after a devastating earthquake and a huge tidal wave sunk most of Lolipolis into the bottom of the sea," said Naleen. "There are still remnants of that sunken city not far from here. Other parts of the city crumbled after many earthquakes and were lost forever under the depths of the sea floor. The few hundred people who survived built this city within the walls of this hard substance that you call a "diamond." It is the largest diamond in the world and the reason why greedy, evil men have tried to come here. They want to crumble the city and take pieces of the outer wall with them. The outer wall is made of the diamond substance and is valuable in your world. It would mean great wealth to those who took it."

"But how does the light from the sun get into the diamond?" Will asked her, amazed by the many particles of reflected light that gave the city an extraordinary brightness and created the deep green color over all the landscape. "And how can we breathe?" he added in an afterthought.

"The sunlight is filtered in through a sophisticated solar system built by the people many centuries ago and the light is reflected off the diamond. But the light comes in only during the day. At night, when the sun goes down, the people use electrical light, fueled by the waterfalls," Naleen explained, as they continued to swim around the first canal towards the great palace. Oxygen is filtered in through a technologically advanced system that scientists of your world have not yet touched upon. That is another reason why men wish to find the city. Technology here is so advanced that it would yield information of great value to your people."

They were coming around the last circle that led to the main island where a great castle was located. Playful dolphins jumped near and greeted them, welcoming them to Lolipolis as they swam through the canal. Katey wished that home was more like this city. Imagine being able to converse with dolphins and whales! She couldn't wait to get home and tell her father. Like Katey, her dad shared a deep love and respect for all animals.

When they arrived at the center island, Naleen bid them goodbye and said she'd be back later. "There is someone waiting to see you in the great castle. I am sure you will be pleased," she said, and then, with a flick of her great tail, she swam off.

Curiosity filled their faces as they looked about the castle, noticing the figures of people who walked toward them now. Smiling and wearing flowing, light clothing and sandals, the people of the Diamond City of Lolipolis greeted them and led them to their leader.

Their leader was a tall, soft-spoken, and wise man who was accompanied by a poised, statuesque woman. "Hello, my children," said the man, whom they learned was named "Grel."

"This is my beautiful wife, Marina," Grel said, as he turned to the woman whose arm was wrapped in his. Marina had kind, bright green eyes and long, shiny red hair. Katey took an instant liking to her. Her gentle manner and kind face was much like her mother's.

"Welcome to our city. I hope your ride here was pleasurable," Grel said. "Naleen always tries to make everyone comfortable, as do many of the whales and dolphins that live here. As you have probably already noticed, we have learned how to communicate with our mammalian friends. Whales are highly intelligent creatures, even more intelligent than you can ever imagine."

He extended his arm to Katey and she took it as they continued to move through the palatial rooms of the castle.

"We learned that whales communicate over vast distances and use various sounds to speak to each other," Grel continued. "We have discovered over time what the patterns of these sounds and songs mean and how to talk to them in their own language. We studied the patterns for many hundreds of years. Did you know, for instance, that whale songs can be heard up to a hundred miles away? It is an extraordinary means of communication at great distances. Even humans cannot do that without the aid of equipment, such as telephones, radio systems or computers."

Will was fascinated by all this information and Katey could almost see the wheels in his brain churning to take it all in. In the meantime, Bartholomew's face, full of amazement, almost made Katey laugh out loud.

"Wow, can someone pinch me please? I think I might still be dreaming," Bartholomew said. At this, Katey burst into laughter. "You should see your face, you look hysterical," Katey said, still laughing at Bartholomew's expression.

"Well, Katey, you might as well wipe that silly grin off your face. It's not as if you don't look like you've just eaten a giant ice cream cone dripping with chocolate," he chirped back, smiling.

Even George looked fascinated, his usual scowl lines softened, as he listened to Grel's words. The entire atmosphere of the city was both soothing and energizing. It pulsed through the entire land—and their very souls.

Grel and Marina continued to show them around the castle, introducing them to many people. The people of Lolipolis seemed to know who they were already, almost as if they were expecting them. A woman with long black hair and clear sky-blue eyes stared at George, a slight smile curving now around her mouth. He nervously smoothed back his hair with his hand and gave her a quick smile before they left the room. They followed Grel into an enormous room.

The room was decorated with paintings of nautical scenes and warm mahogany furniture. A large roll-top desk displaying photos and statues of whales and dolphins were prominent in two corners of the room. The colors in the room were warm green, beige and peach and it radiated a soothing atmosphere. A lamp with a lighthouse at its base gave the room soft hues. The lamps shone constantly and never needed bulbs changed, as did the ones at home. Katey's eyes fell to the desk as she noticed a blue cap sitting on top. Eyes round as giant circles, her heart jumped when she saw the cap. She picked it up, instantly recognizing it.

Before she could say another word, a door to another room opened and out stepped someone who had been in her dreams constantly these last few weeks. She dropped the small statuette of a whale she had picked up to examine and gasped, clasping her hand to her mouth in surprise. Will turned and stopped, frozen in place for one moment in time. In unison, they both shouted, "Uncle Hughie!"

Katey recovered from her surprise and was the first to run into the arms of Uncle Hughie. He picked her up and swooped her around the room in delight. When Will's senses returned, he walked over to Uncle Hughie, his hand extended. Uncle Hughie took it and then grabbed his arm and enfolded him in a great big hug.

They swelled with a feeling of happiness they had not felt in a long time. The tears Katey had been holding back for so long, streamed unabashedly down her face. After they all calmed down, Katey and Will introduced George and Bartholomew to Uncle Hughie. They explained the details of their adventure from the beginning: from when they found themselves washed up on the island where Sharkley found them, to the end, when they escaped the ship and found Whale Island. Uncle Hughie listened intently. Sometimes a sad look filled his eyes and then the twinkle appeared and the contagious laugh when they told him about funny things they did together. Then, donning his cap, he began to tell them how he came to be on Whale Island.

"Well, now," he said, "I'll bet you thought you saw the last of me after the boat capsized in the storm in Cape Cod Bay. I looked everywhere for you, even got the help of Taleki, my old whale friend. Taleki found me bobbing around in the sea, unconscious, my arm and head injured. He brought me to safety. He took me here, of course, where they treated my wounds, which healed in a day. The advanced medical techniques they have are amazing. All wounds heal a hundred times faster than they do at home," Uncle Hughie said.

"When we couldn't find you," he continued, "We learned later that you were kidnapped by Sharkley. We knew that Sharkley was headed for Whale Island. You were always under the protected eyes of the whales and dolphins while you were on Sharkley's ship, of course. I knew you would be okay, especially if you had the whistle. That whistle belonged to my friend, Grĕta, a wise old one hundred three-year-old woman who knew the way to Whale Island. You, see, she fell in love with a sailor and moved to Green Cave Island with him. After he died, he left her as the keeper of the map of Whale Island. She was the only other person, besides her husband and me who ever saw Lolipolis, the lost city. But she was left for dead by Sharkley who found out about the map and stole it from her."

"But, wait a minute, Uncle Hughie," Will said, "How did you find your way to Whale Island without the map?"

"That's a long story," Uncle Hughie began. "You see, many years ago, I saved the life of a whale that was nearly killed by Sharkley and his crew. I nursed this whale back to health and treated her wounds. In return for saving her life, she gave me a whale bone and showed me the power it gave to those who held it in their hands. Then she told me that there are not many of the bones of her forefathers left. She said the bearer of the bones has power to speak to those that live in the sea. She then told me I would be one of them forever. She showed me the way to Whale Island

and the sunken city. From that day forward, I have vowed to help the whales and dolphins, as I have learned how to communicate with them, even without the aid of the bones. I learned, just as the people of the Diamond City of Lolipolis, how to speak to them, work with them, and get along with them here, in a nearly perfect world. This is the world of the Diamond City of Lolipolis."

"Who is the whale you saved, Uncle Hughie?" asked Katey, in wonder and awe of it all.

"Good question, Katey-did. How did I leave that out?" he said, scratching his head. "That would be my dear friend, Naleen, the lovely whale who brought you here and knew that you were on your way. The knower fish at the lagoon told her that you were there. I have been waiting for you," he said. "And, we're going to go home to your father."

"Wow!" said Bartholomew, his mouth wide open the entire time at hearing the astonishing story. Will and Katey knew that this was not one of Uncle Hughie's fantastic or imaginative stories that he sometimes liked to tell after a sea expedition. This was the real thing and it was wonderful.

"But why does Sharkley want to come here so badly? Why would a man who hates whales and kills them want to communicate with them?" asked Will.

Grel interrupted here and in his soft-spoken voice

reminded them what Naleen told them—that the Diamond City is a precious treasure to men of their world. "Lolipolis is called the Diamond City because it is protected by a dome and exterior completely made of diamonds. The whalebones that support it help to protect it, as does the fact that few people of your world know about our city. There have been many theories about Lolipolis, but no one really knows the whole story. It has been kept a carefully guarded secret by our people. If evil people find it, they will destroy it for the sole purpose of taking the diamonds. But they'll have a hard time, and most probably will die before they get here," said Grel.

Now Grel stood up, and took the arm of his wife. "Let us go and enjoy a meal together. You must be hungry and thirsty after the long day. You will each have your own rooms to rest and freshen up. One of my people will call you to dine with us a little bit later. At the sharing of the meal we will discuss the history of my city." At that, he bid them goodbye.

A lean, muscular man with long black hair and confident manner showed them the way to their rooms. Katey's room was adjacent to Will's room. Bartholomew and George's rooms were across the hall. Uncle Hughie's was right next door to Will. He gave them a hug and an affectionate pat on their cheeks and watched as the man led them to their rooms.

Katey felt like she was floating in a dream. Her room was blue and white, with fluffy clouds painted on the ceiling and on the walls, scenes of dolphins swimming in the sea. The large window on one wall overlooked one of the canals, now busy with several boats and whales working alongside the men. She was fascinated by this world and wished her dad could be here to share it with them. But she also knew that she missed him and being home. School would be starting soon, and boy, would she have a great story to share. Of course, they would all think she was making it up and that was okay, because Lolipolis and its people had to remain a secret. Her world was not yet ready to share a beautiful world such as this. She wondered if they would ever be ready. She picked up the stuffed giraffe on the white canopied bed and hugged it. Then she noticed the beautiful, clean clothes that were set out for her on the bed. It would be wonderful to take a real bath and get into new clothes. She looked at the tattered clothes she was wearing, and wondered why she never noticed how raggedy-looking they had become.

After taking a bath in a blue, gold and white bathroom with yellow sparkling tiles and a large clawfooted bathtub,

Katey fell into a deep and pleasant sleep. When she awoke, she stretched and smiled, remembering where they were. It felt so good to sleep in a real bed, she thought. She quickly dressed, brushed out her long auburn hair with the brush and comb on the mirrored vanity and went to find Will.

Will was already dressed and out of his room. He went for a swim in the large pool overlooking the canal. It was filled with sea water and playful dolphins performed their acrobatics, all the while talking to him. The whalebone was attached to his swimsuit as he dove in. Katey worried when Will didn't come up after a few minutes in the water. Then she remembered that he had the whalebone and could stay under for hours. Will was enjoying the playful antics of the dolphins.

Bartholomew was dressed in the light clothing that everyone wore in Lolipolis, a flowing material with almost no weight. His clothes were a vivid blue and green and he sported comfortable sandals on his feet. Katey thought the blue and green made the color of his eyes look even more sparkly-green than usual. He looked handsome in his clean clothes and Katey watched him as he walked over to her.

"Hey, Katey," Bartholomew said, bouncing on the edge of her lounge chair as he watched Will dive into the pool. He nearly landed on top of one of the dolphins, who gracefully moved out of harm's way. "How did you sleep?" Bartholomew asked Katey. "Just like a baby," she said in response, stifling a yawn.

"Me too," said Bartholomew. "I haven't slept so peacefully in ages."

"Grel said he would bring us to the third ring later to see the animals that live there. He says there are no ferocious animals on Lolipolis; all the animals on the ring get along. There's a lot to explore," Bartholomew added. "Do you want to go?" he asked, studying her face, a face that he liked to look at when Katey didn't know he was looking.

Her auburn hair shone brightly in the sunlight. When she looked up, he looked away. "Of course, 'silly head.' I wouldn't miss it for the world!" Katey said. "Where's George?" she asked, wondering where he could be. She hadn't seen him for a few hours now.

"Oh, George is in love," said Bartholomew, laughing and pointing to a large patio that overlooked the canals. "See that brick deck over there? There's a huge dining hall next to it and he's talking to a girl who has been eyeing him since we came to the palace."

She laughed and looked pleased. "I'm happy for George. He needs to have someone like that in his life. I mean, someone other than us, of course."

"What do you mean?" Bartholomew said, feigning a hurt look on his face. "I thought he loved us," and he pretended to cry. Katey gave him an affectionate punch in the arm. They began playing a game of thumb wrestling until Katey, losing most of the games, grabbed his hand in frustration. Laughing, Bartholomew called her a sore loser and tousled her hair.

They both jumped when a spray of water surprised them, landing squarely in their faces. Apparently Will asked a dolphin to splash them. Amused by their expressions, he hooted with laughter and climbed out of the water. The dolphin waved a raised flipper and swam away.

Just then, Balin, the man who showed them to their rooms earlier announced that dinner would be served in the Circular Dining Room in the main palace. He explained how to get there and retreated with a warm smile, leaving them to get ready. Will dried himself and took his clean new clothes with him to the changing room.

When they walked the immense halls of the palace, they were fascinated by each new sight. The richness of the furniture and yet simple grace and elegance of the people here were both comforting and soothing.

They found the Circular Dining Room, which revolved ever so slowly so people could see the three rings of land

and canals surrounding them as they ate. Katey saw Uncle Hughie and walked over to sit with him. His table was next to a huge window that took up an entire wall of the room. You could look out a wall of windows and see all the perfect beauty around them. Chattering happily with Uncle Hughie, Katey noticed that George was sitting next to Kayna, the girl he met earlier. The two were fast becoming friends. George could barely keep his eyes off her. Katey chuckled inwardly when she saw how his face softened when he looked at Kayna, the lines from his usual scowl nearly gone now.

Grel and Marina joined them. The dining room soon filled with people of all sizes and shapes, each wearing the lightweight, flowing material that seemed just right for the temperature and atmosphere of this place. The food was plentiful and the people who served the food were friendly. The colorful food displays on the table made such a wonderful presentation that Katey thought it was too pretty to eat. But it tasted better than any of the food they had eaten on the *Barking Barracuda*. The famished four ate like they hadn't had food in weeks.

Music flowed softly into the room as dancers—men and women—put on a show that mesmerized Uncle Hughie and the children. They moved in graceful, catlike movements to the beat of music that was hypnotizing. They stayed here until the music faded and most of the people had already left the dining area.

Grel was an avid storyteller and enjoyed sharing the history of his world with them. After they had their third round of drinks from cups that automatically filled with the liquid of their choice, he sat back and explained the fascinating history.

"The people of Lolipolis go back in time to more than 9,000 years. In that span of time, we have learned how to eradicate all disease and most people here live to be hundreds of years old. Cosmic science has given us knowledge well beyond the imaginations of the scientists of your world. We have air- and seacraft that your scientists have only begun to imagine, superior to those created by humans and they cannot be destroyed. With our aircraft, we have succeeded in interplanetary and time travel."

"You must realize we are not the only inhabitants in this vast universe. There are other beings living on planets throughout the universe and there are universes that exist in other time warps that can be visited with sophisticated time travel vehicles. You would be truly humbled to see this and know that our Creator keeps watch on all life forms everywhere!" Grel said. He took a sip of his drink, and continued.

"Many thousands of years ago, we learned how to communicate with porpoises and dolphins and naturally, our friends, the whales, became extremely important to us. They are the key to harmony between your people and living creatures that inhabit the vast oceans. One day, your scientists will discover this, as we did."

The revelation that there were other beings from other planets in the universe, as well as universes from the past and future was awe-inspiring to Will and Katey, who were captivated by his words. "To think that you have developed technology so advanced that you have seen other life forms!" Will said. "I want to learn more about the history of Lolipolis."

"You will, in time, Will," Grel said. After dinner, Grel invited them to a common room that would seat a few hundred people. It had a huge floor-to-ceiling television screen that was built directly into the walls, so they felt like they were part of all the scenes from the movie they watched. Three dimensional characters drew them into the plot, as if they were participants of a virtual adventure. When it ended, Uncle Hughie took them to a large library with a fireplace and sat them down to fill them in on what was happening at home.

"You know kids, your father misses you more than anything," Uncle Hughie began. "He spent weeks trying to find you. After you disappeared, police search parties and the Coast Guard were dispatched all over Cape Cod. They conducted investigations, but there was no trace of you. Your father almost lost his mind with grief. He lost a lot of weight and has aged. When I told him that you were with me, he cried like a baby. He was so happy and can't wait to see you again," Uncle Hughie said. "We're going home in two days. I have a small ship and crew, and we'll chart a course for Barnstable the day after tomorrow."

Tears began to stream down Katey's face at hearing the news about her father. She knew he was probably sick with worry. After her mother died last year, it nearly broke his heart. He mustered all of his willpower to come back to them. She was glad that they would be going home soon. Even though this place was wonderful, she missed Dad, her dog, Gobie, and her own room. And she wanted to tell Dad all about this wonderful place.

The next two days were a whirlwind of excitement and wonder for Katey, Will and Bartholomew. They visited the third ring on the outskirts of this extraordinary city and went on a safari tour of the ring that was the largest in Lolipolis. Will blew his whistle and learned that the animals responded to it here too.

A quiet giraffe walked gracefully over to them, its long legs giving her a statuesque appearance. She spoke to them about her family and the baby she was expecting. The giraffe took them into the jungle where other animals lived harmoniously. There, they visited with other giraffes, bears, moose, deer of all sizes, orangutans, chimpanzees, small, cat-size versions of lions and tigers, flying animals, and every animal they had ever heard of, even some they had never seen before.

Katey felt like she was in a dream and thought it was the most amazing day she had ever had in her life. "To be able to speak to these animals was something people only dreamed of and yet we were actually doing it," said Katey, wonder filling her once again at this magnificent place and its people. All too soon, they had to leave and go back to the palace. On the way back, they chattered excitedly about the animals on the third ring.

Just as they were yesterday, new clothes were laid out on the beds in their rooms and they bathed and changed to have breakfast with Grel, Marina and the others. When they arrived at the Circular Dining Room, Uncle Hughie was telling them his sea stories and they listened in amusement and fascination.

Katey's mind drifted to thoughts of home. She wished they could stay longer in this paradise-like place but she wanted to go home. One day, she vowed she would return to the Diamond City of Lolipolis, just as Uncle Hughie did. Maybe they could take the boat and Will's submarine invention and come back in the future. With Naleen and the whalebones, they would find their way back, and they knew she would be a lifelong friend. All they had to do was blow the whistle and she would come for them.

George had already made up his mind to stay in Lolipolis with Kayna. He had fallen madly in love with Kayna and she with him. George wanted to get married and live in the paradise-like home of Lolipolis. Katey would miss her friend, George. She would return one day to visit him, because he would not be able to leave once he made up his mind to stay. It was a decision he made and he was very sure of it.

Katey remembered that the lost city was to be kept secret. Those who lived there could never go back to Katey and Will's world. Few people of Lolipolis ventured out of the underwater city and when they did it was only for supplies, specific food and other necessities. They always came back to Lolipolis. It was like a silent pact among the people and they shared a bond of trust. Only Uncle

Hughie came and went, choosing to live his true life in the world above sea level. He came back to visit the lost city often. He was trusted, loved and respected there, and was a welcome visitor. Grel told Katey, Will and Bartholomew that they would always have a place in Lolipolis. Katey knew it was an honor to be asked back, and her heart burst with happiness at the thought of it.

CHAPTER 15

THE ENCOUNTER

They left the next day, bidding farewell to Grel and Marina, who were saddened by their decision to leave so soon. Katey, Will and Bartholomew made their last stop at the canal to say goodbye to Naleen.

"Remember," said Naleen, "Always keep the whalebones close to you. And, if you ever need to reach me, use your whistle and keep a whalebone at your side. I will come to you. You will always be in my heart," she said, and with that, she lowered her great body into the water, plunged in, her huge fantail waving a final goodbye, until it disappeared into the depths of the canal.

They swam through the tunnel, this time with two whales to accompany them. The whalebones were safely tucked in their pockets; the rest packed away in their knapsacks. The pressure in Katey's chest was not as uncomfortable as the first time they swam through this tunnel. When they finally broke through to the surface, they were back at the mountain with the cave, Uncle Hughie by their side. A ship, sails billowing, was anchored and waiting for them, along with five crew members who would eventually return to Lolipolis.

The ship, called *Mali*, was outfitted with all the supplies they would need to bring them home. They walked up the plank and Katey thought it felt strange, almost like being back at Sharkley's ship. But this was not the *Barking Barracuda*. Katey shuddered at the memory of their weeks on that terrible ship.

Mali, a gray, white and yellow seacraft was named after one of Uncle Hughie's dolphin friends and its mast was shaped like a dolphin. It was clean and everything was meticulous, right down to the floorboards. Katey saw that it was very different from the *Barking Barracuda*. That ship was dark and unfriendly, right down to the drab black and gray colors. This one had a special engine that worked a hundred times more efficiently than any ship at home and it would get them home faster, Grel told them.

They heard a sharp movement in front of them and before they heard the dreaded *click drag* sound, they saw the dark figure. He was holding a gun. With his one black eye gleaming evilly at them, Sharkley now stood directly in front of them, barring them from going further into the ship. He turned his gaze on Uncle Hughie, aiming a .38 pistol at his chest. The cruel smile that always seemed like a cross between a smirk and a frown was turning the corners of his mouth down. Sharkley looked like a mad scientist, his eyes shining with an unnatural light.

"Uncle Hughie, be careful," Katey whispered, moving at once to his side. But Sharkley turned the gun on her. "Move away, missy, or your Uncle will get a bullet in his chest!"

"She means you no harm, Sharkley," said Hughie. Leave the young ones alone," he said, an angry flush appearing on his cheeks. He moved Katey away from the barrel of the gun. She stepped back and her frightened eyes watched as the hateful expression on Sharkley's face grew. She remembered how much he wanted the whalebones and to get to the diamonds of the lost city.

Uncle Hughie's face was contorted with anger as he stared at the madman standing before them, the gun aimed at their chests. "George was right, all along," Katey said.

"You were planning to find us and steal the whalebones."

"Hand over the bones or you'll never see the light of day again," Sharkley said, now pointing the gun at Uncle Hughie's chest. Henshaw had come up behind him and stood at his captain's side. "And I want all of them," Sharkley said, waving the gun at Uncle Hughie. "I knew I'd find you here. You have no clue how much power those bones have. You think you do, but you don't. I know what the bones can do . . . I made that old woman on Green Cave Island tell me everything before I got rid of her," Sharkley said, his black eye twitching at the remembrance.

"You're nothing but a coward, Sharkley," said Uncle Hughie, his face flushed in anger. "That woman was one hundred fifty-three years old. Only a coward could hurt a woman like that."

Sharkley laughed, undisturbed by his comments. "I got to Whale Island just after you did," he continued, ignoring Uncle Hughie's remarks, "but a Komodo dragon nearly killed us, preventing us from getting to the bones in time."

"That mutinous George will have a price to pay for what he did!" he said, now, turning his rage on George. "He'll be sorry he ever saw my face," he said, looking at Hughie with hateful, piercing eyes that bore through him.

Turning his attention on Katey, Will and Bartholomew, he continued his tale.

"When we got here, we couldn't find the bones. But we were sure that you had already stolen them," he explained, looking at Katey. "But I knew that might happen so I had an alternative plan. And that plan worked, because here I am. Now my future is set."

"The bones won't help you, Sharkley," said Uncle Hughie, unruffled by his hateful glare. "You'll use them for evil reasons and that's not what the bones were meant for. They are only useful to those who know their true value. And that has to do with understanding the animals our Creator gave us . . . the animals of the sea and the land. You've killed animals for no good reason and have no understanding or compassion for them. Or for people, for that matter. The bones would work against you," said Uncle Hughie.

"Who are YOU to tell ME that I don't know anything about the bones?" Sharkley shouted, spit flying from his mouth. "You, who thinks you are a great sailor and have no real knowledge of the sea. The sea can be merciless. I know the wrath of the sea. No one knows that better than me. Look at my leg, nearly torn apart by a twenty-two foot shark. It's my time now. And I'll do everything it takes, including getting at those diamonds."

"Yes," he continued, choosing his words carefully and slowly, "I know all about the diamonds of Lolipolis. Why do you think I came here? I intend to have them," he spat out, raising his gun menacingly up toward Uncle Hughie's head.

Just then, a huge whale slammed into the boat. Sharkley stumbled and fell down. The gun flew out of his hand, landing at Katey's feet. Dazed and confused by what had just happened, Henshaw turned too late to see what caused the commotion. In a split second decision, before anyone realized what was happening, Katey scrambled to pick up the gun and handed it to Uncle Hughie. Steadying the gun in his hand, he cocked it and aimed it at Sharkley's head.

"I don't want to have to use this gun, Sharkley," said Uncle Hughie, "so I'm going to send you back to the lagoon. But first, I want your mate's knife and the gun in his pocket. Yes, I know it's there. I'm not stupid. Hand it over," he said to Henshaw, who began to hand it to him. In a swift movement, he plunged at Uncle Hughie with the knife, as Katey's scream filled the air. Realizing what was happening, Uncle Hughie took a step backward and the gun went off, hitting Henshaw in the arm. He fell, grabbing his wounded arm with his other hand.

"Now both of you, get in the water and start swimming

toward the lagoon on the other side of the island."

Sharkley's sharp black eye never left Uncle Hughie's face. He slowly backed up to the rear of the ship. "That goes for you too, Henshaw," Uncle Hughie said, eyeing them both carefully. Hesitating, they waited, but he raised the gun again, aiming it directly at their faces. "Well, gentlemen," said Uncle Hughie, "Jump in or you'll feel the sting of a bullet between your eyes."

At his words, they dove into the water, Sharkley cursing and shouting as he bobbed up and down in the water. "This isn't the last time you'll see me, sailor boy! The next time, you'll be gone before you can count to three!"

Uncle Hughie held the gun steadily at them until they were at a distance far enough away for him to feel comfortable. As they watched, a dark shape raised its white-tipped dorsal fin above the surface, appearing suddenly in the water. It was swimming rapidly toward the retreating bodies of Henshaw and Sharkley. Down went the fin and closed in, meeting its mark. Following a piercing scream, Henshaw disappeared into the depths of the water, dark red circles of blood the only sign of the spot where he had been. Terrified, Sharkley froze in the water. As he gained his senses, he began swimming toward the shore, but not before the shark reappeared and clamped razor-sharp teeth on his leg as he frantically swam away from it. He screamed in pain and fought his way to the shore, dragging his body and mangled leg from the water. Panting, he lay bleeding on the wet sand, blood seeping from the wounded leg.

"You'll be sorry you left me here. You'll never get out of here alive!" Sharkley said desperately, lying on his side in the sand. "If you leave me here to die, you know you won't be able to live with it. Bring me aboard and I'll help you get home," he said, his voice pleading now. He looked pathetic and Katey almost felt sorry for him.

"Find your way back to your ship, Sharkley," Uncle Hughie said. "You'll not be allowed on this one." And with that, Uncle Hughie lifted anchor and headed toward home.

CHAPTER 16

THE JOURNEY HOME

They found the rest of the crew, bound and gagged, but safe, on the deck below. They untied them and Katey, Will and Bartholomew learned their names. They were all unhurt, but a bit shaken. Uncle Hughie gave them something to eat and they rested until their energy and spirits returned. Then he told them what would likely happen to Sharkley. The wretch would most likely be food for some of the animals on the island.

Turning his attention on Katey, Uncle Hughie put his arm around her shoulders, and turned to her to face him.

"Did you know your actions were very courageous,

Katey-did?" Uncle Hughie said, flashing his infectious grin at her. "You saved my life and probably all of us," he added, taking off the blue cap that he always wore, and putting it on Katey's head. "Cap'n, Katey," he said, bowing low and gallantly, "I salute you." The boys followed his direction and did the same. Blushing and bursting with pride, she returned the salute. After what happened today, she knew she was as brave as anyone.

They charted their course toward home and knew the ride would not be short, even with the state-of-the-art technology of the ship. But it was nothing compared to the many weeks they were away on the *Barking Barracuda*.

"Uncle Hughie," Katey said later when they were eating dinner, "I was so afraid that Sharkley would hurt you or even shoot you. I couldn't let him do that to you, not after we just found you again! So when he dropped the gun, I didn't think, I just grabbed it. Naleen arrived at just the right time."

"You are a heroic girl," he said proudly. He tousled her hair affectionately and then she told him about their adventures on Whale Island and their narrow escape from the *Barking Barracuda*. She was eagerly sharing the part about the earthquake that left them all shaking. Then she told him about the time she found Scally's dead body.

"We didn't know who it was because his face looked different, but when we discovered it was Scally, we buried him. It looked like someone hit him over the head and left him there. George said that an animal must have mauled his body after he died," Katey said, remembering how the corpse looked, glad she was far away from that part of the island.

"That poor man probably tried to break away from Sharkley and never made it. Most people who have set out for Whale Island never do and those who are lucky enough to get there just never make it off the island. The man died because of someone else's greed. We don't know for sure how he died, but my guess is that it was Sharkley. Poor Scally probably never saw it coming," Uncle Hughie surmised.

"See, that's what greed does to people. They want money and power, but with wrong intentions, they are doomed. That's one of the reasons why none of the people who did manage to get to Whale Island found the lost city of Lolipolis. The lost city is in harmony with the creatures of the ocean. It's a way of life. And it's very hard for us to understand or to reach those heights. Most people are too greedy for money and power. They misuse the wonderful living creatures God has given us," Uncle Hughie said.

"Is it true, Uncle Hughie, what Naleen told us?" Katey asked him, remembering what Naleen said when she brought them from Whale Island to Lolipolis. "About Green Cave Island being the only other place in the world that leads to the Diamond city?"

"Yes, Katey, that is true," Uncle Hughie said, "but no one but you, Will, Bartholomew and I know about it. You have to promise to keep it that way."

The small ship was equipped with everything they needed to get home safely. Will walked around the ship, examining every piece of equipment. He could run the ship, Katey knew. During the time they spent on Sharkley's ship, he quietly learned all of its intricacies, in case they ever needed to operate a ship themselves. He knew that day might come.

On the voyage home, they stopped at some of the familiar islands that Uncle Hughie visited previously during his ocean travels. They always kept the whalebones with them. Sometimes Will blew his whistle and they would talk to the dolphins that swam close by. Some of the whales surfaced every now and then too.

It would become a way of life for them but no one else could know about it. The people of their world, the "upper world" were not yet ready to communicate with dolphins and whales. One day soon, they hoped the world would be ready.

They were home almost two weeks later, the familiar houses and landscape that made up this part of Barnstable in full view. Katey was filled with excitement as she saw their house set far back from the bay. It was the house where she grew up and it looked the same, the Victorian blue and white house with the white porch that wrapped around the front and sides. As they approached the dock near their home, they saw a tall, thin shape stand up and slowly walk toward them.

"Dad!" Katey shouted with glee. He looked thinner than she remembered, but it was her Dad!

Will and Katey jumped onto the dock after Uncle Hughie anchored the small ship. Katey ran into the arms of her father, hugging him fiercely. Dad looked haggard, his face sunken and eyes marked by a heart-wrenching sadness. He began to cry softly, hugging his children as if he would never let them go again. Katey hated thinking how he must have felt not knowing where or how they were, or even if they were alive.

A cheerful bark came from the porch and the medium-sized brown and black dog quickly ran over to them, tail wagging furiously, jumping up and down in pure joy. Katey kneeled down and hugged Gobie, the lovable dog that greeted her every morning and waited at the door every day until they returned from school. "Gobie, I missed you so much!" She picked her up and let Gobie's wet kisses cover her face.

"How did you get out of the house?" Dad asked Gobie, laughing at the dog, who was wriggling with excitement. Katey giggled while her dog intermittently wriggled back and forth, poured her love on Will, and licked Katey's face with wet kisses.

Dad clasped Uncle Hughie's hand in a hearty handshake and put an arm around his shoulder. "You're a sight for sore eyes," Hughie, said the older brother with affection. They were so glad to see each other after the long separation.

After introducing Bartholomew to Dad, they sat down on the porch and told him the whole story, right from the beginning, to when they found Uncle Hughie on Whale Island. They told him about George, who helped them escape the ship, and how he had fallen in love with a girl on Lolipolis. They spoke excitedly about the power of the whalebones and why holding them enabled them to speak to the animals. They explained in detail the lost city that was enclosed in a huge diamond. Dad was listening quietly, amazed that they had escaped from Sharkley's cruelty and found their way to this mysterious island.

"That's quite a remarkable story!" Dad exclaimed, looking at their faces in awe. "You have no idea how much I missed you." He turned to the lean youngster who seemed a bit timid in his new surroundings. "Bartholomew, thank you for your help—especially for getting Will and Katey off the ship." He noticed the affection Katey and Will had for Bartholomew and realized they shared a close bond.

"You can stay with us for as long as you want. We have plenty of room and we could use the company. Of course, you'll have chores to do, the same as Katey and Will," he said, a small smile mischievously playing around his mouth.

"Dad makes us work hard. You'll have to clean the bathrooms and scrub every tile on the floor," Katey said, "Oh, and you have to make all the beds. I used to do that too. Oh, yes, and the dishes every night, of course." And then, she and Will burst out laughing at Bartholomew, who was surprised at first, but soon replaced the look with a big grin. Katey couldn't resist teasing him.

Bartholomew was beginning to feel comfortable in his new surroundings. *This is probably what it feels like to be part of a real family*, he thought. It was very different from life on the *Barking Barracuda*.

After many hours of talking and laughing, Uncle Hughie excused himself and left, telling them he'd return on the weekend. "Great to be home, kids, right?" he said with a wink, and then left, whistling. They ordered pizza, Katey and Will's favorite food. Bartholomew had eaten pizza only a few times in his entire life. Katey and Will described it as the best food in the world.

"I can't believe you only had pizza once or twice in your life, Bartholomew. As for me, I'm going to eat pizza every day for two weeks, until school starts," Will said, his mouth already drooling at the thought.

After they were finished eating, Will showed Bartholomew around, ending the tour in the garage to show him his newest invention, the submarine that never made it to the water. "Wow, this is the coolest sub I've ever seen," exclaimed Bartholomew.

The trio decided they would put it in the water this weekend. That was just two days away.

On Saturday, Will got the submarine ready and Uncle Hughie came over to help hook up the sub to the boat. They would be going back to Green Cave Island, complete with their whalebones and Will's whistle. This time, if they found the knower fish, they would use the bones to talk to them.

As they boarded the boat, Katey wondered if they would find the way to Lolipolis from Green Cave Island. Green Cave was the shortcut to Lolipolis. Only Uncle Hughie and the knower fish knew the way. The only other person who had known was Grĕta, Uncle Hughie's friend who was never seen again. She was planning to meet Uncle Hughie there to give him important information about the whales near Australia. But then, Sharkley found her and the map.

Uncle Hughie saved whales on his marine expeditions. He had several whalebones and always kept one with him. Like Will, Katey and Bartholomew, the whalebones helped him to breathe under water. He learned when a whale or dolphin was hurt or injured and rescued them.

As they approached the cove at Green Cave Island, Katey's mind flashed back to the day of the big storm, and the voyage home that felt like a strange dream. She recalled that day as if it was yesterday. *All those days on the Barking Barracuda with that horrible Sharkley, and then on Whale Island…it's amazing that we are here to talk about it*, thought Katey. Everything seemed different today. Maybe it was because she felt older and knew so much more than she did just weeks ago.

A few days later, they took Will's submarine to the bay.

It was one of the best days of their lives. They tied their whalebones around their waist and stayed underwater for hours, knowing the bones would help them breathe.

They didn't go back to Lolipolis that fall, as they originally planned. But they did find Naleen and the news that she gave them was surprising. Sharkley was alive and had somehow escaped from Whale Island! Naleen thought he must have had help but didn't know how he managed to get off the island. Grel and Marina were made aware of the news and took measures to protect Lolipolis. Will, Katey and Bartholomew knew that they too would have to be extra careful.

One early March morning when the sun was streaming through the kitchen windows and they were getting ready to go to school, Katey, Will and Bartholomew made a pact that they would return to Lolipolis in a few months when the weather turned warm. They didn't mention it to Uncle Hughie but the trio longed to go back.

Clasping hands, one on top of the other, they vowed that their next adventure would happen in June. And this time, they knew they would be ready.

ABOUT THE AUTHOR

Karen Bonnet grew up in New York and lives with her family on Long Island. Her love of reading began as a young girl when she delighted in all books, especially the *Nancy Drew* series, the *Bobbsey Twins*, *Pippi Longstocking*, and many classic novels, such *The Wizard of Oz*, and Mark Twain's *Tom Sawyer* and *Huckleberry Finn*. Her favorite children's book was *Carbonel: The King of the Cats* by Barbara Sleigh.

As an adult, she worked in administrative positions until she began her career as an editor/reporter in the early 1990s. She wrote numerous articles for community newspapers and several magazines. As a published author, her articles and photographs appeared in well-known regional news publications, trade papers, and magazines. Later, she became involved in public relations, working for schools, and a nationally-recognized nonprofit.

She eventually turned to entrepreneurship and is a co-partner of KLB Services/The Nonprofit Solution, a company that offers expertise in all facets of nonprofit management, public relations, and marketing.

Karen has been married for thirty-four years, and has three accomplished children, and a two-year-old granddaughter. Her educational credits include a Bachelor of Science degree from SUNY Empire College; she is an honorary member of the Phi Theta Kappa Society at Nassau Community College.

WHALE ISLAND . . .

For more information regarding Karen L. Bonnet
and her work, email her at: kbonnet@optonline.net
or visit her website: www.karenbonnet.com or
blog: www.whaleislandstories.wordpress.com.

Additional copies of this book may be purchased
online from LegworkTeam.com; Amazon.com;
BarnesandNoble.com or via the author's website,
www.karenbonnet.com.

You can also obtain a copy of this book by visiting
L.I. Books Bookstore
80 Davids Drive, Suite One
Hauppauge, NY 11788
Or ordering it from your favorite bookstore.

Breinigsville, PA USA
31 January 2011
254421BV00005B/2/P